T0221707

CHRISTMAS IN BETHEL

CHRISTMAS IN BETHEL

RICHARD PAUL EVANS

G

Gallery Books

New York   London   Toronto   Sydney   New Delhi

Gallery Books
An Imprint of Simon & Schuster, LLC
1230 Avenue of the Americas
New York, NY 10020

First Gallery Books hardcover edition November 2024

GALLERY BOOKS and colophon are registered trademarks of Simon & Schuster, LLC

Simon & Schuster: Celebrating 100 Years of Publishing in 2024

For information about special discounts for bulk purchases, please contact Simon & Schuster Special Sales at 1-866-506-1949 or business@simonandschuster.com.

The Simon & Schuster Speakers Bureau can bring authors to your live event. For more information, or to book an event, contact the Simon & Schuster Speakers Bureau at 1-866-248-3049 or visit our website at www.simonspeakers.com.

Interior design by Erika R. Genova

Manufactured in the United States of America

10 9 8 7 6 5 4 3 2 1

Library of Congress Cataloging-in-Publication Data

ISBN 978-1-6680-1488-2
ISBN 978-1-6680-1489-9 (ebook)

To Laurie Liss

CHRISTMAS IN BETHEL

PROLOGUE

Please don't judge me too harshly. The jury in my own head is merciless enough and rarely adjourns.

Beth Stilton's Diary

Despite the title of this book, my story is more of a love story than a Christmas story. I hope that's okay with you. Especially since most Christmas stories *are* love stories. I don't think that's a coincidence. Christmas, if done right, is love. And love, like Christmas, should be infused with magic.

I've been accused of oversharing, but I think it's the things we don't share that people really want to hear. And if I can't be honest, I might as well write fantasy, which, I admit, my story still feels like. Things like this don't happen to ordinary people. Especially me. Up until that Christmas, my life was a dumpster fire, but without the warmth or illumination.

I'll warn you in advance that I'll be sharing a few difficult parts from my past. I have to. If I left the hard parts out, there would be no story. And you wouldn't believe it anyway. Only lives on social media don't have problems.

Most of the time I feel like I live in a different world than the rest of humanity—like I march to the beat of a different cellist. I don't participate in popular culture, I don't have a subscription to any streaming services, I don't recognize the faces on magazine covers, and the only music I listen to was composed before our century or was meant to be played on vinyl records.

The one exception to my cultural detachment is books.

There are authors who somehow speak my world's dialect. Or at least my heart's. So, I suppose it's not entirely surprising that what happened to me that Christmas unveiled more like a novel than real life, and involved an author. Most of all I wonder why he chose me.

My name is Leigh, though I go by my middle name, Beth. There are two reasons for that. First, as Leigh people assume I'm a man, which sometimes has its advantages, but usually just makes me feel masculine. Second, because Lee was my biological father's name, whom I don't want anything to do with. I think my mother named me Leigh hoping that my father would feel some attachment and stick around. It worked for only a little while.

My last name is Stilton, like the cheese. Enough said.

That was a lot just to tell you my name. I'm thirty-nine, though I look closer to thirty, I have dark brown eyes and middle-of-the-back-length, cappuccino-colored hair, and I'm five foot six. Men tell me that I'm pretty, but since that's all they seem to care about, I stopped seeing that as a positive. These days I don't do much to be pretty. I'd as soon wear a ball cap than do something to my hair. And since I mostly work at home, shaving my legs requires a command performance.

I'm single, by choice, because I have poor judgment in men. I'm apparently attracted to narcissistic abusers. The thing about narcissists is that they're charming on the outside, but once the veneer has worn off, there's nothing but anger. I've never known a narcissist who wasn't rageful at his core.

The thing about narcissists is that you're either a supporting actor in their play or a prop. And if a prop isn't where they want it, they'll just kick it out of the way. That's all I've been in my life—a prop in others' dramas. I've wondered if I subconsciously sought out these men because that's all I thought I deserved. Up until that Christmas season, it was all I'd known.

I suppose that I was groomed for failure. My father left us when I was two. When I was nine, my mother, who was a mean-spirited alcoholic, married a man who abused me until I was fourteen. When I was eleven, I told my mother what he was doing to me and she slapped me and called me a liar, so I kept to myself and silently endured the nightmare. I had an older brother, but he was smart—he'd left as soon as he could.

My only escape at that time was books. I read voraciously. I read everything they had for young adults, which, back then, was two shelves in the public library. Then I read them again. By the time I was ten I had read *Gone with the Wind* twice.

When I was in the eighth grade, Mrs. Johnson, my middle school gym teacher, saw me in the shower, and I was called in to the school office. I had no idea what I'd done, but I was left with a school counselor who interrogated me until I confessed to what was happening at home. I was terrified. I thought I was in trouble—like, go-to-jail trouble. I wasn't, at least not from the authorities, but my stepfather was. He was arrested. My mother never forgave me for that. I suppose I never forgave her either. I don't know who I hated more, my stepfather for what he did to me or my mother for letting him do it.

Unwanted, I left home at sixteen. I got a job with a wilderness rescue team. I found three bodies that year, all of them suicides. It was the beginning of a new kind of trauma in my life, one that never left. A year later, I became the youngest EMT in Pennsylvania. That's also where I met my first boyfriend, Lance. Handsome, cocky Lance. He was my boss; a twenty-six-year-old thrill junkie, and I was his underaged thrill. The day I turned eighteen he took me out to celebrate my birthday, though he was really just celebrating himself. He took what he wanted. It took only three months for him to move on.

I had some dark experiences as an EMT, even more than I'd had on the rescue team. Car and motorcycle crashes, burn victims, murders and suicides, things most people see only on TV. It's different when it's real. They collected in my head like a shelf of bad movies, sneaking out of my subconscious in the form of night terrors. By the time I was eighteen, I had seen more horror than most people will witness in their entire lives. The things I saw still haunt me. I sometimes wake at night screaming.

After Lance, I moved on the only way I could think of and joined the military. That's where I met my husband, Dan. He was large and muscular, and I guess that's what attracted me to him. I assumed he could protect me. Unfortunately, there was no one to protect me from him. Once he started beating me, there was little I could do.

I got pregnant seven months after our marriage. One night, angry that I was pregnant (as if he hadn't anything to do with that) and too sick to cook his dinner, he threw me down the stairs. I lost the baby I was carrying. I was still in the hospital when I filed for divorce. By the age of twenty-two I was divorced, had lost a baby, and was alone with a mind filled with more horror than a Stephen King movie marathon. Like I said, dumpster fire.

That's when I got the idea to find my birth father. I don't know what I was looking for; probably some misguided hope for connection or salvation. Or maybe something more basic, like validation for my existence. One of the books I read when I was younger was about a young woman hunting down her birth father and their happy, somewhat comical reunion. I think I bought into the fantasy. Unfortunately, the book version was different than my reality.

Ronald Jeffrey Lee (I know, it sounds like a serial killer's name) wasn't happy to see me. That's putting it mildly. He started with denial, basically telling me that I didn't exist and asked to see my birth certificate, which I don't happen to carry around with me. I think my body is proof enough that I was born. Then, when he saw that I wasn't backing down, he said, "What do you want? I don't have any money."

That was obvious. He dressed like he didn't have a mirror either. His socks didn't match, he wore a wife-beater T-shirt, and his hair—what was left of it—looked like it hadn't been washed or combed since George Bush was president (either Bush). I found him at home in a low-income housing unit in the middle of the day with a beer in his hand. The man was a living stereotype.

He proceeded to tell me that I was a mistake and that he wished I had never been born. I told him that at least we agreed on one thing.

I meant that. I really did wish I had never been born. Alone, broken, and unwanted, I had nothing left to live for.

That's when I decided to end my pathetic little life. I knew that no one would miss me. Outside of my brother, whom I never saw, I couldn't think of even one person who would care. I set a date for December 25. It would be a Christmas present to myself. In a deeply macabre state of mind, I even bought one of those cardboard Advent calendars, the kind that have a chocolate behind each day's door, and began counting down the days to my departure.

During those "coda" days I found myself wandering a lot, both mentally and literally, mixing with the bustle of holiday crowds. I was in a bookstore looking for something to distract myself when I came across a book titled *Bethel* by an author I'd heard of but never read: J. D. Harper. I don't know why, amid all those book-laden shelves, this book called out to me. Maybe it was some spiritual force that guided me to this book, or maybe it was just the echo of my name in the title. Whatever the reason, I bought the book and took it home to start reading.

I didn't sleep that night. The book felt as if it had been written just for me. The way the author wrote, it was like he knew me, like he knew my pain and walked with me. This was someone who understood loss and brokenness. This was someone I could trust.

I sniffled through the last half of the book, and cried when I closed it. Something in me had changed. I felt purged and new, like not only had I found someone who cared for me but, for the first time in my life, I was worthy of being cared for. I wanted to be loved the way this author wrote about love.

I knew he was a big-time author. I'm sure millions of people felt the same way about him as I did, but I put that out of my mind. He was mine. Just mine. He wrote just for me.

I threw away the Advent calendar. (After taking out all the chocolates, of course). And then I went back and found everything Mr. Harper had written. At the time there were seven books in all, each as powerful as the first. I read and reread them until their pages were worn.

Life went on. Significantly, *my* life went on. I no longer thought about ending it. The days crawled, but the years flew. I changed apartments; I changed careers.

Then, more than a decade after I found that first book, I read in the paper that J. D. Harper was coming to my town for a book signing. I had to meet him. I wanted to look into the eyes of the man who could conceive such things. I had to know if he was real.

I planned for more than three weeks for that day. I bought a new outfit. Two of them. Truthfully, I was as terrified as I was excited. What if he wasn't anything like his books? How could a man that successful not be affected by fame and fortune?

But my greatest fear was personal. What if meeting my author was as disappointing as meeting my father had been? Then I'd no longer even have the comfort of his words. I almost didn't go. But in the end, my curiosity was stronger than my fear. It was time to meet my author.

CHAPTER

ONE

Up until then, my only accidental encounters involved fenders and insurance companies.

Beth Stilton's Diary

I look kind of cute, I thought, glancing over my shoulder at the hall mirror before walking out the front door of my home. It had been a while since I tried to look anything besides legally clothed. I was dressed casually in my favorite faded jeans and a mid-length cardigan sweater made of alpaca wool. I suppose it was a little weird dressing up for a book signing. What was I hoping for? That my author would find me attractive? Or recognize me as the one he'd written the book for? I'd clearly read too much fiction.

Even though the signing went only until noon, I had taken the entire day off from work.

My author had never been through Pennsylvania before, at least not on a book tour, so I guessed, correctly, that the line for the signing would be long. I knew that the mall opened an hour early for walkers, so I strategically arrived at the mall before that, thinking I would slide in with the silver sneakers club and beat the rush. About three hundred people had the same idea. When the door opened, the crowd rushed to the bookstore, a few openly sprinting. It was like the running of the bulls in Pamplona. One woman fell, and no one stopped to help her. I would have, but before I reached her she was up and off like an Olympic athlete.

The bookstore's overhead gate was still closed, but the

lights were on and there was a table set up at the front of the store with a poster of the new book. I waited in line for a bit, when the woman next to me said she could really use a coffee. I was thinking the same thing, so I made a deal with her that I'd get us both coffee if she'd save our place. She gladly agreed and I went off to the mall Starbucks, about fifty yards from the bookstore.

"Lee," a sleep-deprived-looking barista said dully, setting a cardboard coffee cup on the counter. As I went to get my coffee, another man, about my age, stepped forward and took it. He was attractive, moderately built with short, combed-back hair. He was wearing a casual shirt printed with newspaper headlines of UFO sightings. As he turned away, I said, "Excuse me. I think that's mine."

He turned to me. "Are you talking to me?"

"Yes, I believe that's my coffee."

He looked down at the cup. "It's my name."

"Mine too," I said. "Did you have a white-chocolate mocha?"

"Definitely not." He looked at the writing on the side of the cup. "No, you're right." He handed it to me. "Sorry. I just heard my name called."

"Do you take other people's bags at the airport too?"

He grinned as he looked into my eyes. He had beautiful blue eyes. "Only if they have my name on them."

Then one of the workers set a cup down on the counter. "Lee."

"That one must be mine." He took the cup and read the label. "Yes, that's mine."

Just then a couple sitting at a small table near me stood. The man moved for it. "Pardon me, could I take your table?"

"Of course," the woman said.

He sat down in one of the chairs, then looked up at me. "Care to join me?"

I glanced around to see if there was anything else, but the place was full. "Yes. Thank you."

He looked amused. "Are you sure?"

"Very." I set my purse and coffee on the table, then sat down.

"I'd introduce myself," I said, "but that's already been done."

"Then we can skip the pleasantries," he said.

"That's a cool shirt," I said.

He glanced down at it. "I know. I saw it at Nordstrom and I had to get it. It looks gangster."

"That's what you're going for? Gangster?"

"I do what I can." Suddenly his smile vanished. I noticed he was staring at my arm. "What does your tattoo say?" he asked.

I pulled back my sleeve and showed him my arm.

So it goes.

"Vonnegut," he said. "*Slaughterhouse Five*. Great book."

"In fifteen years, you're the first person who's got that right."

"It's the ultimate existential phrase."

"It was my sad existential phase," I said.

"Do you have any other tattoos?"

I don't know why but I showed him my other arm. "This one."

There is no spoon.

"From *The Matrix*," he said. "Challenging the belief that there is reality outside our perception."

"Two for two. I'm truly impressed."

"What phase of life was that?"

"My Keanu Reeves phase."

He grinned. "That's funny. Any others?"

"Now you're prying."

"If you weren't so accommodating, I wouldn't be."

I held up my wrist to reveal a cross.

†

"What phase is that?"

"My current one."

He nodded. "It's a bit more hopeful."

"What about you?" I asked. "Any tats?"

"I've got a few markings, nothing I could show you here."

"Markings?"

"More of a brand."

"Like from the Marines?"

"Something like that," he said. He went back to his coffee.

"What are you drinking?" I asked.

"Caffè americano with milk. And my own addition." He took a small bottle of energy drink from his shirt pocket and poured it into his cup. When he was finished, he looked up at me. "You're staring."

"Do you always drink your coffee with an energy shot?"

He took a drink. "I call it jet fuel—enough octane to wake the dead. And it's cheaper than crystal meth."

"It doesn't give you the jitters?"

He held out his hand. "Nope. Steady as a rock."

"What about your heart?"

He grinned. "It's been through worse." He took another drink of his caffeine. I tried to hide how disgusting it was to me. I drank my coffee instead.

I don't know what it was about him that made me so chatty. Maybe his shirt. "Do you work here in the mall?"

"No. Do you?"

"No. I'm here for a book signing."

He set down his coffee. "You mean that line outside the bookstore."

"I know, it's massive. I'll probably be here for hours."

"Probably. Who's the author?"

"J. D. Harper. Have you heard of him?"

"I have."

I patted the bag I was carrying. "His new book came out four days ago."

"It's in your bag?"

"Yes."

"May I see it?"

I took my book out and handed it to him.

"*Winter in Arcadia*," he said, reading its title. "It has a nice cover."

"I like his covers. They've got their own, kind of, retro style. I hear they're making a movie from this book."

"A movie, huh?" He turned the book over. "No picture of the author."

"No, it's like his thing. No pictures."

"That's unusual. Authors are usually publicity hounds. So you don't know what he looks like?"

"Well, sort of. There are pictures of him posted by fans on the internet."

He closed the book. "You just bought it?"

"No, I couldn't wait that long. I got it the morning it came out. I've already read it. In fact, I'm halfway through reading it again. . . ."

He handed the book back. "Was it any good?"

"Like I said, I started reading it again, so that's kind of a clue."

"Or maybe you hoped it would end differently the second time."

"Isn't that the definition of insanity, doing the same thing hoping for a different result?"

"Insanity, no," he said. "Stupidity, maybe."

"Well, the book was amazing," I said.

"Amazing. That's a strong word. What was so amazing about it?"

I thought about it. "I guess it's the way it made me feel. Like the rest of his books."

"How was that?"

"It's hard to explain. Sort of like I'm alone with the author." I bit my lip. "Does that sound weird?"

He shrugged. "A little."

"Haven't you ever read something that made you feel that way?"

"Not the kind of things I read."

"What do you read?"

"Contracts, mostly."

"You're a lawyer?"

"No. But when I read for pleasure it's mostly nonfiction. Tank battles of World War II. The Civil War. Things they make documentaries from. I loved Stephen Ambrose."

"I'd rather read the back of a cereal box."

"I didn't mock your taste in books."

"No, you mocked me."

"When did I do that?"

"When you agreed I was weird."

"I'm sorry," he said. "But you set me up for that." He took a long drink of his coffee, glanced down at his watch, then said, "I'll even the score. Here's something weird about me. I collect pewter Civil War figurines."

"I didn't know there was such a thing."

"There's a society of collectors." He studied my reaction, then said, "You're looking at me like I'm a freak."

"No, it's just . . . you don't strike me as that kind of person."

"What kind of person?"

"Someone who collects little figurine things."

"You're making me sound like a loser."

"I didn't mean that. It's just, you look put together."

"Yes, you're definitely making me sound like a loser. What does *put together* have to do with collecting figurines? People collect all sorts of things. Some of these soldiers go for thousands of dollars."

"I'm sorry. I didn't mean to insult you."

"Everyone collects something," he said. "What do you collect?"

"Regrets, mostly."

He laughed. "What else do you collect?"

"Books," I said. "I've got enough for a small library."

"Who do you read? Besides this guy?"

"I used to read Mary Higgins Clark before she passed away. I read Nicholas Sparks, Nora Roberts."

"Big-time authors."

"Like Mr. Harper." I looked back over at the line, which had nearly doubled since I'd sat down, and there was still fifteen minutes before the signing even started. "That line is insane. People were waiting outside for hours."

He glanced over at the line. "Shouldn't you be saving your place in line? I don't think it's getting any shorter."

"Someone's holding my place. I told her I'd bring her a coffee if she'd hold my spot."

"You got the better end of the deal," he said. He took another drink. "I've never understood why people queue up like that. They do it for electronics too. It's always on the news, people sleeping out for the new iPhone or video game. Why not just go the next day and buy it?"

"You've never waited in line for anything?"

"Only for my driver's license. I avoid crowds whenever possible."

"Book signings are different. It's like bringing the author home with you. When I was a teenager, I slept overnight at a record store to get a signed Barry Manilow record."

"Barry Manilow. And you made fun of me for collecting figurines."

"I was a kid then. It was more about getting out of the house. But this is my first time waiting in line for an author."

"What is it about this author's books that would make you stand in that line?"

I thought for a moment, then said, "It's kind of personal."

"Books should be personal. Any reason in particular?"

I took a deep breath. "In my early twenties I had just left an abusive marriage. I had no family. I had just lost a baby. I had no job, no home. I had no one. Then, unfathomably, I decided to find my biological father. I still don't know what I was looking for."

"Home," he said. "I think we're all looking for home."

His words struck me hard. After a moment I said, "Whatever it was, I didn't find it. He said I was a mistake and wished I had never been born. I agreed with him. I decided to end my life on Christmas Day."

His expression turned deeply sympathetic. "Why Christmas Day?"

"I don't know. It just seemed right."

"I'm sorry," he said. "But you're still here. What changed your mind?"

"He did. J. D. Harper. That's when I found one of his books."

He pointed to the line. "That author?"

I nodded. "The book was *Bethel*. It was the first time I felt like someone understood what I'd been through. It spoke to my very core. I think, mostly, I felt hope." I paused to fight the emotion rising inside my chest. "I've read every book of his since then."

"I can see why you read him," he said.

I suddenly felt like I'd come out of a trance. "I'm sorry. I don't know why I just spilled everything out like that to a stranger."

"We do that," he said. "We're all wanting to connect some- how." He smiled. "Even with a stranger."

"Maybe," I said. "Thank you for listening or whatever."

"Thanks for sharing. No wonder you're so excited to meet your author. I would be too. You didn't tell me your last name."

"Stilton," I said.

"Like the cheese?"

"Like the cheese."

He glanced down at his watch, then said, "I need to get to an appointment, but . . . would you like to go to dinner with me?"

The invitation surprised me. "That's kind of you," I said. "But I'll have to say no."

He frowned. "That's disappointing. You're already in a re- lationship?"

"No. And I'm hoping to keep it that way."

"Well, just so we're clear, I wasn't asking for a relationship. Just dinner."

"You just felt the need to feed a random stranger?"

"An interesting and attractive stranger. Why not? Besides, I give to all sorts of charities that feed people." He stopped. "You're really not interested, are you?"

"It's nothing personal."

"I'll tell my ego that."

"I mean, it's all personal, just not personal about you. You seem very interesting, and yes, you're very attractive. I've just had a bad run with men lately. And by lately, I mean forever."

He slightly nodded. "I'm sorry."

I smiled sadly. "Me too. You seem very kind. But so did the last one."

"So it goes," he said, grinning wryly. He finished his coffee, then stood. "All right. But if you change your mind, you'll know where to find me."

"I will?"

He just smiled. "Have a nice day, Leigh. It's been a pleasure getting to know you."

"You too," I said softly. I watched him toss his cup in a waste receptacle, then walk off. I sighed. He really did seem like a nice guy.

CHAPTER

TWO

The interesting thing about waiting in queues is that you never know who you'll meet besides the person you came to meet.

Beth Stilton's Diary

I finished my coffee, went back to the Starbucks counter and ordered a cappuccino grande for the woman who was holding my place, then took it back to her.

"Here you go," I said.

"That took a while. I was starting to wonder if you'd skipped out on me."

"No. I drank mine in the café."

"By the way, my name is Kathy," she said, extending her hand.

"Beth."

"Do you know if he'll sign his earlier books or just the new one?" On the ground next to Kathy was a canvas Trader Joe's shopping bag filled with books.

"I think the paper said he's just signing the new book."

She groaned loudly. "And I lugged these all the way here. I swear it's like fifty pounds."

"I wish I had brought another book," I said to her. "I only brought one. Everyone else here has stacks."

"They have them at the table," she said. "If they don't sell out. How long have you been reading J.D.?"

"About ten years."

"I started a little before that," she said. "I came across *Jacob's Ladder*, then I got *Bethel*. Then the rest of them. I've already read this one twice. I'm going to read it again when I get home. I told my husband, you better pick up some tacos on your way home from work, because I'm not cooking."

"*Bethel* was the first book of his I read."

"That one broke me open in a million pieces, you know?"

I nodded. It made me a little sad to hear this. A part of me wanted to believe that it was only me who was so affected.

"Seriously, I don't know how this man does it."

"Have you met him before?" I asked.

"Once. I was in Jacksonville, Florida, on vacation. When I found out he had a book signing in Miami, I drove all the way there. That's five hours each way."

"Was it worth it?"

I could tell from her smile. "I'd drive a thousand miles more."

"He was nice?"

"He's such a gentleman. I mean, the people around him rush you through, but he makes you feel like you're the only one at the signing. I know he'd sign all my books if I reminded him about Miami."

"You think he'll remember? I'm sure he meets a lot of people."

"He might. We'll see."

It was more than an hour later when we were finally close enough to the store to see some action. There were so many people around my author, and they had bent the line around a mall display so you couldn't see him until you were almost next in line.

As we stepped forward, Kathy squealed. "He's so handsome. I swear he gets better looking with age."

That's when I saw him. He was seated in the middle of a long wooden table with people on both sides of him moving the books. He was bent over, signing a book, so I didn't see his face right off, but I immediately recognized the shirt. J. D. Harper was Lee from the coffee shop. When he looked up, someone pulled the book from him, while the other woman shoved a stack of open books toward him. That's when he saw me. An amused smile crossed his face. He winked.

"I'm so nervous," Kathy said. "Which one of us was first?"

"You go before me," I said. "You were here first."

"Thank you. Wish me luck."

"Good luck," I said.

"Next!" shouted a young, ubiquitously tattooed woman.

Kathy walked up to the table with her bag of books. I could see the staff telling her their signing policy, but, as she predicted, he just waved the books on and signed all of them. She was still talking to him when someone literally pushed her away.

"Next," the tattooed woman said.

I walked up to him with my one book. "Hello, Lee."

He smiled. "It's good to see you again."

"Your book please, ma'am," a woman said curtly. I handed her my book.

"Is Lee really your name?"

"Lee is my real name. J. D. Harper is my pen name."

The woman opened my book and slid it to him.

"You know, you could have saved me two hours and signed my book at the table."

"I could have. But then there was no guarantee that I'd

see you again." He held up his pen. "Would you like this signed to you?"

"Yes, please."

"Would that be to Leigh or someone else?"

"I go by Beth," I said. "But you can sign it to Leigh. Since that's the name that brought us together." I was talking too much.

A young, pixie-haired woman standing slightly behind him stepped forward. "Ma'am, we need to keep this line moving."

I looked over at her. "Sorry."

Lee glanced over. "It's okay, Carlie. She's a friend of mine." He looked back at me. "Are you still not available for dinner?"

I felt embarrassed that I'd turned down his offer. I'm sure that didn't happen often. "Is the offer still open?"

"It's open. Even though I'm not happy you want to go to dinner with J. D. Harper and not just Lee. Lee's a pretty good guy."

"I'm sure he is," I said. "For the record, I don't care about the famous author part. I want to meet the man who wrote those words that saved my life."

"That was the right thing to say," he said. "I have a speaking event at seven, so it will have to be early. Would five be too early?"

"I'm flexible. Where should we meet?"

"I'll consult with my publicist. Give me your phone number, I'll call when I'm through."

"Mr. Harper," the short-haired lady said, "the natives are restless."

"They'll wait," he said bluntly.

"I'm sorry," I said. I quickly scrawled down my phone number. "Here."

He read my number out loud, then, handing me my book, said, "I'll call you."

"Oh. I wanted to get another book."

"I'll bring one to dinner. It's a guarantee you won't stand me up."

"Like that's going to happen."

I started to walk away. "Oh, Beth," he called after me.

I turned back.

"Thank you."

I smiled as I stepped away from the table. After I was away from the crowd, I opened my book to see what he'd written.

To Leigh,
We'll always have Starbucks.
JD Harper

It was cute, even though he had horrible handwriting. I wondered if he really would call.

CHAPTER

THREE

Wine lubricates the tongue.

Beth Stilton's Diary

He never called. His assistant did. She said they'd meet me at five o'clock at an Italian restaurant called Celeste, the C pronounced *Ch* as in Italian. I'd been there just once. It meant I had to dress up, or at least wear something better than what I'd worn to the signing.

I got to the restaurant a few minutes late, as there was more traffic than I expected, likely due to early holiday shopping and a light drift of snow that had started falling shortly after noon.

When I opened the restaurant door, my author was standing in front of the maître d stand with two other women, one of whom I recognized from the book signing. I felt a twinge of disappointment, since I'd hoped it would be just the two of us. His back was to me as he was signing a menu for the maître d'. He handed the menu back, then the woman from the book signing said something to him, and he turned back. He smiled when he saw me. I walked up to him. "You made it."

"Did you doubt?"

"You never know." He gestured to the woman I recognized from the book signing. "I think you met Carlie earlier."

She slightly nodded. "I was the one telling you to hurry up. Sorry. It's my job."

I said, "He gets to be the hero while you're the scary one pushing people through the line."

"He *is* the hero, and I am the scary one," she said.

"You had me scared," I said.

"Carlie's my personal assistant," Lee said.

"I'm sorry, I didn't catch your name," Carlie said.

Lee said, "That's because I'm not sure what to call her." He turned to me. "Is it Leigh or Beth?"

"My friends call me Beth," I said.

"Beth it is," he said. "It will definitely be less confusing in the long run." He motioned to a woman standing next to Carlie. "And this beautiful woman is Natalie." She was older and taller than Carlie, with bright red hair and gaudy jewelry.

"It's nice to meet you," she said.

"My pleasure."

"Natalie is our local media escort. She takes us around to the television and radio stations, book signings, and events."

"We're going to grab something to eat," Carlie said. "We should be on the road by six fifteen. No later."

"You're not joining us?" I asked.

"No. But thank you," she said flatly. "Good night."

After the two of them walked out of the restaurant, Lee turned back to me. "You said you've been here before?"

I nodded. "Once."

"Just once?"

"It's a little pricey."

"Are you ready, Mr. Harper?" the hostess asked.

"We are."

"Right this way, please." We followed her to the back corner of the restaurant. It was a smaller, more private area and one of the few tables next to a window that overlooked the garden. I suspected it was reserved for special guests. Lee helped me with my chair, then sat down across from me.

"Your waiter tonight is Alfredo," she said. "He'll be right with you."

"Thank you," Lee said.

"I thought Alfredo was a sauce," I said.

He laughed. "And so much more. *Alfredo* is from Old English and translates to 'elf counselor.' Ergo, our waiter is a saucy elf counselor."

He wasn't disappointing.

Alfredo walked up to us. He looked very Italian.

"Buona sera," he said with a thick Italian accent. "Could I interest you in some wine this evening?"

"Would you like some wine?" Lee asked.

"A glass of red?"

"We'd like the Castello di Monsanto, please." He turned to me. "Or would you prefer a Bordeaux?"

"Is it legal to drink French wine in an Italian restaurant?"

He smiled. "Apparently. It's on their wine list."

"Whatever you choose."

"We'll have the Bordeaux," he said to the waiter.

"A very good choice," the waiter said. "Would you like an antipasto to begin your meal? Perhaps some bruschetta or calamari?"

He turned to me. "What would you like?"

"I'm good with anything."

"You're being a little too easy." He asked the waiter, "Is your melon good this time of the year?"

"Very. It's very sweet."

"We'll have the *prosciutto e melone* and the burrata."

"Very good choices," he said. "I will get your wine and be back in a moment."

After he walked away, Lee asked, "Do you think he compliments you on whatever you order?"

"I don't know, but you're two for two."

"Beginner's luck." Lee looked back down at his menu. "You've been here before, what do you recommend?"

"I liked their house special, the Celeste fettuccini with pepper and truffle slices."

"Is it white or black truffle?"

"I didn't know there was more than one kind."

He put down his menu. "I'll have that."

"What if it's the wrong truffle?"

"There is no wrong truffle."

A young woman placed some sliced bread with small dishes of oil on our table. Lee offered me the bread, then took a piece for himself. He poured olive oil and balsamic vinegar on his plate and dipped the bread in it.

Understandably, I was much more self-conscious now that I knew who he was. It was easier when I thought of him as just a fellow Starbucks client. I started with something innocuous. "Are all your book signings as big as the one this morning?"

He shook his head. "No. Some are bigger. Some smaller. It depends on the city. You'd think that the bigger the city, the bigger the signing, but that's not always true. The thing is, in big cities people get a bit jaded. I was signing books in downtown Manhattan, and the line was about a third of what it was this morning. The store manager apologized and said that Mick Jagger had been through the day before. Suddenly, I didn't seem like that big of a deal."

"I can see that."

"That I'm not that big of a deal?"

"No. I meant . . ."

He laughed. "I'm kidding. But it's a thing. Las Vegas is the same way. It's difficult to get media because of all the stars. The last time I was there I got bumped from a radio interview because Mike Tyson walked into the studio."

"Bumped by Mike Tyson."

"I suppose it's better than being hit by Tyson." He grinned. "It could have been worse. It could have been Barry Manilow."

"I don't think it would hurt as much to be hit by Barry Manilow."

He laughed. "I think not."

Alfredo returned with our wine, pouring a small amount into Lee's glass. Lee sniffed it, then nodded. Alfredo filled my glass halfway, then Lee's, then left us with the bottle. I tried the wine. "That's delicious."

"That is good." He took the bottle and looked at the label. "I'll have to remember that."

I set down my glass. "Here's a question. What's the strangest thing you've had happen at a book signing?"

"The strangest . . . I could write a book on book signings," he said. "But the strangest thing . . ." He thought for a few seconds then said, "I've got it. Once, I was in a small town in southern Ohio. I must have been the biggest thing ever to come through, because I'm not exaggerating, the whole town turned up. The line went six blocks down Main Street. The people at the front of the line had been waiting there for twelve hours."

"How did you know that?"

"She told me. You'd be surprised what people tell me."

"I shaved my legs for your signing," I confessed. "I can't believe I just told you that."

He smiled. "You made my point."

"Now I'm embarrassed. Continue with your story, please."

"So, the bookstore was herding people through the line like cattle."

"Like this morning."

"Worse. It was completely hands on, drag people away. While I'm signing, I notice that there's this woman sitting on a chair about ten feet across from the table. She was older, maybe late seventies. But what caught my attention was that she had gauze wrapped around her head, and her hair was matted down on one side with what looked like blood. It was stuck to her head.

"I asked the bookstore owner what the woman's story was. She casually said, 'Oh, that's Gretta. She was in a car accident on the way here. They put her in the back of an ambulance, but she jumped out and came here instead. She said she was feeling a little faint, so we let her sit here until her time in line came.'

"I said, 'You're kidding me, right?'

"'You're her favorite author and she won't leave until she gets them signed.'

"I said, 'Please bring her over here so I can sign her books and she can go to the hospital. No, strike that. I'll go to her.' I got up and walked over and signed her books. I would have driven her to the hospital myself if I had to."

I shook my head. "Fans."

"I love my fans," he said. He looked at me for a moment, then asked, "Are you a fan?"

"I'm not a stalker, if that's what you're getting at."

"I didn't ask if you're a stalker. I asked if you're a fan."

"Who do you consider a fan?"

"Someone who shaves her legs before a book signing."

"I don't think that's what it says in the dictionary."

"What does it say in the dictionary?"

"I'll look it up." I pulled it up on my phone. "A fan or fanatic is someone who likes a thing, a person, or an idea."

"That's not a good definition," he said. "I could like Brussels sprouts, but that doesn't make me a fan."

"You like Brussels sprouts?"

"No, they're foul. Look up another definition."

"Okay, Fan. Noun. First definition: 'an enthusiastic devotee, usually of a sport or a performing art, usually as a spectator.'" I looked at him. "Is writing a performing art?"

"Probably depends on the author."

"Second definition: 'an ardent admirer or enthusiast (as of a celebrity or a pursuit).'" I smiled at him. "Based on that, I am a fan. I am an admirer of your work."

"Thank you."

"And I shaved my legs."

Alfredo brought us our appetizers and took our entrée orders. We both got the Celeste fettucine.

"Have you had this before?" he asked, holding a knife and fork to one of the appetizers—a ripe slice of cantaloupe wrapped in prosciutto ham.

"No."

"It's a great combination." He cut me a piece and put it on my plate.

I tried it while he watched in anticipation. "That is good."

"It's one of my personal favorites. I also love dates stuffed with blue cheese."

We both ate a little, then he said, "Tell me about Beth."

"I think I told you everything over coffee."

"You read me the flap copy; tell me about the book."

"Where should I begin?"

"Where do you work?"

"I work as a fraud analyst for an ACH provider."

"You catch bad guys."

"You could say that."

"Do you go into an office?"

"Once a month. After Covid we all just started working from home. My productivity actually went up, so they told me I could work from home."

"Is it lonely?"

"My whole life is lonely."

"No pets?"

"Up until a year ago I had a dog. A bichon."

"One of those little dogs."

"She was fun-sized."

"You said *had* and *was*. What happened to her?"

"A year ago, I opened the door to get a package and she ran out into the street in front of a car."

"I'm sorry. How long did you have her?"

"Six years."

"That's hard."

"I mourned her hard. Dogs are little angels. It's like they know things. Like when you're sad, or when you're hurting. I had knee surgery a few years ago. When I came home, Puppins kept licking my knee where I'd been operated on."

"Your dog's name was Puppins?"

"Mary Puppins. Puppins for short."

He smiled. "That's pretty cute."

"My point is, I had pants on, so she couldn't see where they'd operated."

"She probably smelled the bandage."

"Thanks for taking that magic away from me."

He laughed.

"Have you ever had a dog?" I asked.

"I have. She was my best friend. In fact, it's one of the saddest stories in my life."

"Tell me."

"Well, it was a difficult time of my life. Not as bad as yours, but not good. Daisy, that was her name, was my only friend. One morning before school, my mother told me to call the dog in. Daisy was across the street when I called her. I didn't see that a car was coming. She ran under its wheels.

I ran over to her and picked her up. She licked my face, then she died in my arms."

"That may be the saddest thing I've ever heard."

"You know what the worst part was? When I carried her home, my mother was mad because I was late for school. She said, 'Put that thing down. You can bury it after school.'"

"What was wrong with her?"

"That's a conversation in itself."

"I'm sorry," I said.

I noticed him furtively glance down at his watch.

"Who are you speaking to, and what are you speaking about tonight?" I asked.

"It's sponsored by the Franklin and Marshall Alumni Association, so I'll be speaking to whoever wants to come. I'll be talking about my book."

"Do you like to speak in public?"

"I do. Before I was a writer, I was in publicity, so it's kind of my forte." He looked at me. "Would you like to come?"

"I don't have a ticket."

"I'm your ticket."

"Then I would love to go."

He smiled. "You can come with me."

"I can drive. I have my car."

"Why would we waste that time we could have together?"

"It's not a problem."

He looked at me as if he was studying me, then said, "That's right. You've been hurt by men. Let me reassure you. We won't be alone, Carlie and Natalie will be with us, and after the event I'll bring you straight back to your car."

I felt embarrassed. "Okay. Thank you."

He seemed happy with that. Just then a pretty, thirty-something woman with short blond hair walked up to our table. She was trembling.

"Mr. Harper, I'm so sorry for interrupting your dinner." Her eyes were welling up. "I just wanted to thank you for all the hours of enjoyment and escape you've given me. You're my favorite writer."

"Thank you," he said.

She looked at me. "I'm sorry to disturb your dinner." She turned and walked away.

"Does it still feel good to hear that?" I asked.

"Every time."

"Does that happen often?"

He nodded. "Fairly often. Sometimes I just hear my name, like I'm in their conversation. Carlie's more attuned to that kind of thing than I am."

"Does it ever get annoying?"

"It depends on the circumstance. And the person's demeanor. This young lady was very sweet and apologetic. And she apologized to you as well; that's rare. Once I was in an intense conversation with my film agent and this woman kept trying to talk to me. My agent lost it on her. It was ugly." He frowned. "To them it's one time, but to me it's every day. That's the difference."

"You lead a strange life," I said.

"I have a good life. I'm blessed."

"What does your blessed life hold for tomorrow?" I asked.

"The tour goes on. I have some early morning media, then some personal things before I leave town. How about you?"

"Usual drudgery for us mere mortals. I have work, I need to go grocery shopping and do some laundry. But I do have my book club tomorrow night. And, coincidentally, we're reviewing your new book."

"But my book just came out."

"I'm sure everyone's already read it. They're all big fans of yours."

"What are you going to say about my book?"

"I'm going to tell them that *Winter in Arcadia* flows like a prized wine, with notes of McEwan and Hosseini, leaving the reader deliriously happy and thirsty for more."

"You're quoting the blurb off the back of the book."

"I was just checking to see if you read your own PR. What should I say?"

"How did the book make you feel when you read it?"

"Sad. It made me cry. Especially when Nicole died."

"Good. Sad sells."

"I'm sure you're right, but I don't understand it. Isn't there enough sadness in life without seeking it out?"

"There's a lot of speculation about that. But look how attentive you were when I was telling you about my dog."

"That's true."

"Some psychologists say it's the same reason we like hot peppers. The pain releases endorphins, which causes pleasurable feelings and numbs our pain. But I think it's more than that. I think, more than anything, we want to feel. Sad stories make us feel more alive. It's a way to experience sadness and catharsis, without the real-life anxiety or stress.

"One of the magazines asked me why I wrote stories that made people cry. I told them, 'I don't write to make people cry, I write to make them feel again.' But as I thought about it, I realized that the books that most impacted my childhood were the books that made me cry. *Charlotte's Web, Old Yeller, Where the Red Fern Grows*."

"Two of those books are about dogs," I said. "And I cried at those too."

"We all did. The thing is, writing a story is like falling in love. You think you're pulling the strings until you discover you're really the puppet."

I liked that.

He continued. "I think what's most important isn't whether the story is happy or sad, but that the ending is appropriate. That's how it was in *Winter*."

"You're saying that you really didn't know from the beginning that Nicole was going to die?"

"I didn't. I didn't want her to. I like happy endings. Of course, I'll get hate mail for sure."

"You get hate mail?"

"Hate mail. Threats. We keep a file of unhappy readers called, *If I ever go missing*.

"That's not funny," I said.

"It's life in public," he said. "But back to the book . . . you could still call it a happy ending. Nicole was finally free from her pain, and Alan was a better man for knowing her. Isn't that happy?"

"It's not the happy ending your readers want. Everyone wants to see them together, happily ever after."

"That's why they call it fiction."

"You don't think people can stay together happily?"

"They can, but only if they change the reason they're together."

"What do you mean?"

"It's human nature. People rarely keep doing things for the same reason they started them. That includes marriage."

"Did your parents stay married?"

"Their relationship was about as temporary as a parking lot fireworks stand. And just as volatile. And your father left you."

"You remembered."

"I have a good memory for detail. Do you want to talk about it?"

I shook my head. "No."

"Fair enough." He took a drink of wine. Our waiter arrived with our food.

Lee said, "Buon appetito," then took a fork to the pasta. I waited for his reaction.

"Is it good?"

"Very," he said. "White truffles."

We ate a little in silence.

"Does your book club have a name?" he asked.

"The Bordeaux Babes Book Club."

He nodded approvingly. "I like that. And here we have Bordeaux wine for dinner. Coincidence? I think not."

"It's fate," I said.

"Would you like some more fate?"

"Please."

He filled my glass, then reached down and lifted the book he'd brought in. "I didn't forget that extra book I promised. Who would you like it signed to?"

"Her name is Pauline. She's hosting the party at her house."

He scribbled in the book, talking as he wrote, "'To Pauline, you are a lovely woman with impeccable taste in books. Thanks for reading. From Beth's friend, J. D. Harper.'" He looked up. "How's that?"

"She'll love it."

He handed me the book. "How big is your book club?"

"We have about eighteen members, but only a dozen of us show up every month. We have a website."

"You have a website?"

"We were just going to have a Facebook page, but one of our members does websites, so it was kind of a no-brainer. We post the books we're reading, our calendar, make refreshment assignments. You're welcome to come. I'm sure they won't mind."

He grinned. "Thank you, but I think I'm already booked."

"Shame. I could have really impressed them."

Just then Carlie walked up to our table. "We need to leave in fifteen."

"Thank you. Would you take care of our bill?"

"Of course. The car's out front."

"Thank you."

Carlie glanced at me, then walked away. I recognized the possessiveness in her eyes.

"She looks after you," I said.

"Yes, she does."

"Like a prison guard."

He laughed. "Good simile."

"Is she married?"

"Just to her job."

"That makes sense. She has feelings for you."

He looked a little uncomfortable. "I know."

I began to push back from the table. "We should go."

He held up his hand. "Don't let her ruffle you. We still have a few minutes. Let's finish our wine."

CHAPTER

FOUR

My author is charming with people, in the plural and singular. I think it's a rare gift, to be the same person behind the curtain that you are on stage.

Beth Stilton's Diary

The ride to the event was pleasant. Lee, Carlie, Natalie, and I rode in the back of a stretch limo, the kind with a lighted bar on one side and a long bench seat on the other.

Lee and I sat together and shared a tiramisu while Carlie and Natalie sat in the front of the compartment facing us. For most of the ride Carlie was on her phone confirming media for Lee's next tour stops. Natalie read the new book, occasionally looking up at us.

After finishing our dessert, Lee laid himself out along the vertical bench and, to my surprise, fell asleep. For a moment Carlie and I just looked at each other. Then she said, "Tours are exhausting."

"I can imagine."

"Being up for his readers takes a toll. To them it's one experience that they'll go back and post on social media. To him, it's one of thousands. They forget that."

"Does he . . ." I stopped.

Her eyebrows raised. "Yes?"

"Nothing," I said. I was going to ask if he often singled out women to spend time with him, then realized how bad that sounded.

Lee slept until we were about ten minutes out. He sat

up and rubbed his face with his hands. Without him asking, Carlie handed him an energy drink.

"Thank you," he said. He opened the drink, then said to me, "Sorry to leave you. I needed a rest before I went back into the lion's den."

"I don't know how you keep up this pace."

"That's what the energy drinks are for."

"Someday your heart will explode."

"I can only hope," he said.

The limo stopped in front of a redbrick building where we were met by several university officials.

"I'm Vance Smith, and this is my wife, Veronica."

"Mr. Smith is the president of the Franklin and Marshall Alumni Association," Carlie said.

"Glad to meet you both," Lee said.

Carlie handed Lee a copy of his book, which he presented to Mrs. Smith.

"Thank you. Would you sign it?"

"I already did."

"My friends will be green with envy," she said.

"Green friends are good to have," he said.

"You've got a great turnout," Mr. Smith said to Lee. "The auditorium holds almost a thousand people, and every seat is filled. And we still have a line of hundreds outside the building. We're setting up screens in two of the other halls. They'll be able to watch the televised event."

"Is that them over there?"

"Yes. Some have been waiting for hours."

Lee walked over to the long line of people. It was obvious when they recognized him because the excitement in the line was palpable. He moved down the line shaking hands and taking pictures with fans, working the crowd like a politician on Election Day.

"Does he always greet his fans like that?" I asked Carlie.

She nodded. "Always."

After he had walked the line, we went inside the building. There was a row of reserved seats near the front of the auditorium. I sat between Carlie and Mrs. Smith.

Mr. Smith stood and introduced Lee, who emerged from the side of the auditorium to loud applause. He shook hands with Mr. Smith, then gripped the lectern.

I noticed that he glanced down at me before he began. I don't know what it was, but I felt a flush of warmth come over me.

"It's a pleasure to be with you here tonight," he began. "Books are a powerful thing. Every revolution began with a book."

He spoke to a captivated audience for about forty-five minutes, then turned the time over for questions and answers. There were microphones in both lanes of the auditorium, and lines quickly formed behind them. I couldn't help but notice how charming he was with the public.

"He knows his readers," I said.

"He loves his readers," Carlie said.

They closed the event at 9:00. People hurried to the stage for autographs, but the handlers pulled Lee out the back door to where the car was waiting. Carlie, Natalie, and I joined him around the side.

"You were exceptional tonight," Carlie said to him. "As usual."

"Thank you," Lee said. He asked me, "What did you think?"

"I think exceptional's a good word."

"Natalie?"

"Exceptional. Brilliant. Extraordinary, I could get a thesaurus if you like."

"Now you're just pandering to my need for validation."

"That's exactly what I was doing," Natalie said, nodding.

"Not me," Carlie said. "I meant it."

"That's totally pandering," Lee said. "What about you, Beth? Pandering?"

"Maybe. I'll have to think about it." I furrowed my brow. "But they did like you..."

He grinned. "Let me know." Then he said, "It's time for Worst Question."

"What's that?" I asked.

Carlie looked at me with a droll smile. "It's a game we play after speaking events."

"All right," Lee said. "My personal candidate for worst question was 'Briefs or boxers?'"

"I thought that was pretty tactless," I said.

"Stunningly inappropriate," Carlie said.

Natalie said, "Runner-up, I'd say it was the woman who asked why you weren't married and then added that she was single."

"We get that every time," Carlie said. "Usually more than once, just stated differently." She turned to Lee. "That and 'Can I have your phone number?'"

"People really ask that?" I asked.

"Always. And there's 'How much money do you make?'"

I turned to Lee. "How do you answer that?"

"I usually just say, 'too much.'"

"That's a good answer," Natalie said.

"Vague answers are always best," Carlie said. "Though it's not like they couldn't look it up. It's out there. *Publishers Weekly* is always posting big advances."

"I don't really think the marriage question was odd," I said. "I think a lot of people wonder that. You're handsome, smart, rich, and famous."

"The marriage thing isn't about him," Carlie said shortly. "It's them."

I wasn't sure what she meant by that.

I said, "I think the worst question was that woman who asked if you would help her write her book. And I liked your answer: 'If I did, it wouldn't be your book.'"

Carlie said, "The crowd liked that answer. She didn't."

Natalie said, "How about that emotional woman who asked how you knew that she needed to hear those words?"

The car was silent for a moment, then I said, "I thought that was sweet."

Lee glanced at me. Then he said, "So did I."

Natalie looked embarrassed. That ended the game. We rode a little more before Lee put his mouth to my ear and asked if I would like to lay my head on his shoulder.

I surprised myself by replying, "Yes." I lay back and closed my eyes. Then he put an arm around me. It felt beautiful. The ambient sounds of the car and traffic dissolved into pink noise as I disappeared in his sphere. I wanted to stay there forever.

Forever wasn't long enough. I could tell when the car left the expressway, the sound of the blinker juxtapositioned with the sound of his heartbeat. I knew we were getting close to the restaurant, and I felt heaviness seeping into my chest. It had been so long since I'd been held or hugged by anyone. I snuggled more into him.

I opened my eyes as the limo pulled into a mostly empty parking lot. "That's my car over there," I said, pointing at my Volkswagen.

"Carlie," Lee said, "tell him it's the Volkswagen."

She knocked on the window that separated us from the driver and pointed at my car. "The Volkswagen."

The driver stopped the limo in front of my car and opened the door for me. I looked at Lee, but felt awkward saying my goodbye in front of Natalie and Carlie.

Before I could say anything, he said, "I'll get out with you."

"We've got an early morning remote," Carlie said as he moved toward the door.

Lee didn't respond. He climbed out of the car first and helped me out, then shut the door behind us. "I'll walk you to your car," he said. "Make sure there's not a rapist in your back seat."

"That was random."

"Just keeping you safe."

We stopped in front of my car, just a couple feet separating us.

"I had a really a wonderful evening," I said. "Unexpected, but wonderful."

"The best times usually are."

"They'll never believe me at book club."

"Probably not."

"May I ask you a candidate for worst question?"

He smiled. "Of course."

"Why me? There are a million women out there who are younger and prettier and madly in love with you. Why did you ask me out?"

"Why not you?"

"I just told you."

"Yeah, the younger and prettier thing." He shook his head. "I'll be the judge of that."

"Younger isn't subjective."

"Its relevance is." After a minute he asked, "Worst question candidate for you. You said you always wanted to meet me. Was it what you expected?"

I smiled. "It was better than I possibly could have imagined. It was a beautiful fiction."

"Fiction," he said softly. "Is that what this is?"

"Maybe. I don't really know what this is. It's not my usual storyline."

He seemed to be lost in his thoughts when he said, "Is there anything I could do to make the story better?"

I swallowed, gathering my courage. "The protagonist could kiss the girl good night."

He just looked at me.

I suddenly felt embarrassed. "I'm sorry, I shouldn't have . . ."

He stepped forward and pressed his lips to mine. After he stepped back, we both were quiet. My eyes began to water, and I looked down. "Thank you."

"Thank you, Beth. I had a wonderful night. The best in a very long time." Then he said, "Would it be okay if I called you again?"

I was still looking down, trying to avoid eye contact, but I nodded.

He breathed out slowly. "I better go. Let me see you safe in your car . . ."

"That's right," I said. "The rapist." I looked up at him and we kissed again. Then I unlocked my car and got in. I rolled the window down. "No rapists."

"Good night, Beth," he said.

"Good night, Lee. J.D."

"Lee," he said. He looked at me for a moment more, then slowly turned and walked back to the limo. I started my car but didn't back out. I just sat there. I felt like I'd just walked through a dream. Had it been? Had my dream author really kissed me?

The limo was already gone when I realized that I'd left my book behind. I'd been excited to give Pauline the book and to impress the Babes. It would have been nice to be the impresser instead of the impressed, for once.

As I drove home, I honestly had no idea what to think of the evening. I wondered if he would really ever call. I wondered if I was really falling in love with someone I'd never see again.

CHAPTER

FIVE

Alice was our book club's moderator tonight. I'm proud of her, fighting her fear of being herself and owning her voice. Maxine was her usual self. Too much self, too much voice.

Beth Stilton's Diary

The Bordeaux Babes Book Club met on the first Wednesday of each month. I had been a member for nearly three years. I learned of the club from a lobby bulletin post at church, and I probably wouldn't have given it much thought, except the book they were reviewing that month was one of J. D. Harper's. I was actively trying to be less of a hermit, so, in a rare show of extroversion, I showed up at that meeting. I enjoyed it so much, I hadn't missed one since.

The club was started about two and a half years before I joined and consisted of eighteen women, twelve of whom were regulars like me. Our name had come from the first meeting where the hostess and club founder, Shelley Winder, had served two bottles of expensive Bordeaux wine she had in her cellar. Even though the club was established as a democracy, Shelley was still the acknowledged queen of the Babes. She was the oldest member of the group, smart, kind, and witty, the widow of a carpet-and-flooring magnate with showrooms in Pennsylvania and New Jersey. She deserved the respect she commanded.

There remained controversy over who had named the club. The founding members agreed that it was Kim Disera who had come up with the club's original name, though Maxine Eggers vehemently claimed the title, which was on par for Maxine's ego. Since Kim didn't care whose idea it was, she let Maxine hold the honor.

I suppose that most book clubs have someone like Maxine—the know-it-all who monopolizes the conversation and talks over everyone who shares an opinion different from hers. Twenty-plus years ago Maxine wrote a book called *MANHUNT: A Newly Divorced Woman's Guide to Dating*. The book was published by a small, local publisher. She had her fifteen minutes of fame with an appearance on the local morning and noon news and a place on a local bestseller's list for one week, so she now thought herself a bestselling author, celebrity, and expert on the entire book world.

Three months after I joined the group, Maxine tried to change our name to the 6 B's Book Club, which stood for The Bordeaux Busy-Body Brilliant Babes Book Club, but everyone agreed that people would think that the 6 B's referred to the honey-producing flying pollinator instead of the second letter of the alphabet and people would assume there were only six of us and that we were "beelike," whatever that meant. It was also pointed out that technically, using the words *book club* at the end of 6 B's Book Club was redundant. Maxine sulked through the rest of the meeting, but we all stood resolute in our position.

We chose our books from the *New York Times* bestseller lists, though we occasionally strayed to culturally relevant topics and upcoming books from favorite authors, such as Nora Roberts and J. D. Harper. J.D. was the one author we universally loved—except for Maxine, who insisted that he was a formulaic writer of common skill. I don't know why she would say that, except to make herself look smarter than us, so when Shelley reminded her that Mr. Harper's second book, *Jacob's Ladder*, had been a National Book Award finalist, she mumbled something about the book awards being political and that her book had gotten a nod from the committee but had been surreptitiously shot down by fanatic Christians. We let at least half of what Maxine said just roll over us. The other half we ignored.

Books and pleasant company were just part of the club's appeal. There was also the wine. I'm not a wine connoisseur, but Bordeaux is a pretty great wine. People who are paid to describe wine describe Bordeaux's flavor as pencil shavings (really?), sage, cedar, violets, spices, and minerality with fruit notes of currants, plums, and cherries. Up until joining the book club, I had tried a Bordeaux only once. It was one of the cheaper brands, but I remembered liking it.

We had developed a tradition of sorts; while our taste in books remained constant throughout the year, our choice in Bordeaux varied. Our club's high point was a 2021 Lafite-Rothschild Bordeaux at $700 that Shelley had bought at a charity auction, which we all just sniffed and sipped a small bit, then talked a lot about.

This month's meeting was held at Pauline Barrett's home. Pauline, one of the club's founders, was a displaced Texan belle about ten years older than me, as sweet as pecan pie and about as nuts, which meant that I adored her. She had made her great-grandmother's coffee cake, which was reason enough to come. I was still kicking myself for leaving the autographed copy of Lee's book for her in the limo. I debated telling her about it. But the more I thought about it, the more I thought I'd sound like I was just making it up.

Shelley had brought the wine this time; each month someone brought a case of twelve bottles, a bottle apiece. That might seem excessive, but it's what we went through, though I usually limited myself to two glasses and brought the rest home.

Pauline's home was older, but of gorgeous art deco design; it was large, tastefully furnished, and immaculately kept. (Shelley told us that Frank Lloyd Wright had been involved in the architecture, which Pauline hadn't told us since she was afraid that it might appear boastful.) Pauline and her late husband collected valuable art, and there were original paintings and sculptures scattered around the house. I once asked her why she hadn't remarried, and she just said she didn't have time for that kind of nonsense, though she did have gentlemen friends whom she occasionally traveled with.

Each monthly meeting was moderated by a different member, which gave each of the dozen active members the chance once a year. My next turn was three months away. This month's facilitator was a newer member named Alice Liddel. She was a friend of Carol Lewes, a former club member who had moved away shortly after I joined. Alice was such an introvert that we assumed she'd stop coming after her friend left, and we were all pleasantly surprised when she was there the next meeting. The moderator's duty was to present three books from which we'd each vote on. Then, at the next meeting, to bring a biography of the author and back information on the book before opening the meeting up for discussion.

Like I said, we were all surprised when Alice agreed to take her turn at facilitating a meeting. We knew this was a huge leap for her, and we were all pulling for her. In many ways I related more to Alice than the others. Up until her arrival, they would have said that I was the quiet one in the group.

Alice had typed her notes on one sheet of paper, which she shyly hid behind.

"Today's book . . ."

"A little louder, honey," Shelley said kindly. "We can't hear you over here."

"Sorry." She cleared her throat. "Today's book is titled *Winter in Arcadia* by the bestselling author J. D. Harper. Mr. Harper burst the publishing scene in 2003 with *Jacob's Ladder*, which climbed the *New York Times* bestseller list to the number one spot, was a National Book Award nominee, and has since sold more than nine million copies in thirty-seven countries. A major Hollywood movie starring Gary Oldman and Helen Mirren was made from the book.

"*Jacob's Ladder* was Mr. Harper's second book. His first book, *Bethel*, had been released two years earlier, but, like many debut works, received very little attention. After the success of *Jacob's Ladder*, *Bethel* was rereleased by its publisher and also became a major bestseller.

"*New York Times* reviewer Jennifer Wu wrote: Had the introduction of the two books been reversed, I believe that *Bethel* would have likely been even better received than its remarkably popular successor."

"Mr. Harper was born in Huntsville, Alabama, though he lived in more than a dozen different cities before attending college at Emory University in Atlanta, Georgia."

"They've got a stellar creative writing program over there," Maxine blurted out. "Some rank it as the number two writing program in the country, just below Columbia in New York."

Alice looked at her as if waiting for permission to proceed.

"Continue," Shelley said.

Alice cleared her throat again. "Mr. Harper." She swallowed, then started again. "Before becoming a bestselling author, Mr. Harper worked at Porter Novelli of Atlanta, an award-winning global public relations firm with offices in more than sixty countries."

Maxine said, "PR firms and advertising agencies put out more writers than an Alabama distillery. Law schools do, too. If you think about it—"

"Good lawd," Shelley said. "Let the woman speak."

"I'm just adding color," Maxine said.

"She's colorful enough, thank you," Shelley said. She turned to Alice. "Go on, dear."

"Thank you." Alice looked back down at her sheet. "*Winter in Arcadia* is Mr. Harper's ninth novel." She looked up, glancing around at us for approval.

"That was just lovely, dear," Shelley said. "Very nicely done."

"Lovely indeed," Pauline echoed. The rest of us joined in with a chorus of approval.

"Now, how did you feel about the book?" Shelley asked.

Alice breathed in slowly. "I thought it was really good. But I thought it was sad. The ending was sad."

Maxine started, "The thing about—"

"Wait your turn," Shelley said.

Maxine shut her mouth. The rest of us furtively glanced back and forth, hiding our amusement. Shelley didn't take guff.

Shelley asked Alice, "What is it, for you, that made it sad?"

"Well, because I wished that Alan and Nicole could have ended up together." She looked around the circle. "But I still thought it was a very good story with a powerful message about loyalty and self-sacrifice." She paused for a moment, then said, "I've always wanted to feel loved the way that Alan loved Nicole."

"Amen to that," Kim said.

"You nailed it," Deborah, a blond-haired former beauty queen, said. "Seriously, at one point, I had to stop reading because I was overheating like an automobile's radiator in August." Then she added, "But the ending with Nicole, I didn't see that coming. It was like a sucker punch to the gut."

"I hear that," someone said.

Alice glanced down at her notes, then boldly asked, "Why do you think the author ended the story that way?"

Maxine, sufficiently humbled now, raised her hand, looking at Shelley, not Alice.

Shelley nodded and Alice said, "Yes, Maxine."

"Moolah."

"Moolah?" LaVonne said, her face scrunching up like a re-cycled can. "What does *moolah* have to do with anything?"

"Money is the blood of the publishing world, honey. It's all about sales. Authors write stories that make people cry. If they cry, they buy. End of story."

The room turned quiet. Once again Maxine thought she'd schooled us. J. D. Harper was a sellout. It made me angry.

"That's not why he wrote the ending the way he did," I said, making a fairly rare appearance.

Everyone turned to me.

"Oh? Tell us your theory," Maxine said.

I glared back at her. "It's not a theory. He said that stories sometimes just follow their own path. He didn't want Nicole to die either, but the story dictated it. He said that writing stories is like falling in love. You think you're pulling the strings until you realize you're the puppet."

"Like falling in love," Pauline said. "Isn't that man just a poet?"

"That totally sounds like something he'd say," Deborah said, nodding.

"Where did you read that?" Maxine asked.

"I didn't read it. He told me that."

"*Who* told you that?"

"He did. Lee. I mean J.D." Then I added, "Harper."

"J. D. Harper told you how he wrote his book?"

"No. He just told me that he didn't want Nicole to die. And a few other things."

"Well," she said, sitting back in her chair. "Now that we know that you and J. D. Harper are BFFs, what else did he share with you?"

"Take it easy," Kim said. "She went to his book signing."

"And since she was the only one at the signing, he had lots of time to talk to her about books, the weather, and whatever."

"Maxine, leave her alone," Shelley said.

"We're here to talk about this book, and if J. D. Harper himself gave Miss Beth some special insight, I think we'd be remiss to not let her share it."

I looked over at Alice, who looked as terrified as a cashier at gunpoint.

I smiled reassuringly at her, then I said to Maxine, "It wasn't at the book signing. It was at dinner. He took me to dinner."

A peculiar frost came over the group.

"J. D. Harper took you to dinner?" Kim asked.

Now everyone looked unsure as to whether to believe me or not. I couldn't blame them. I hardly believed it myself.

"This just keeps getting better," Maxine said. "Then what?"

"I went with him to his speaking event at F&M," I said.

"I tried to get tickets to that," Deborah said. "It was sold out."

Maxine raised her eyebrows. "And then, back to his hotel?"

"I'm not going to talk any more about this," I said.

There was a pause in the conversation, then Alice said, "Does anyone else have something to add to our discussion?"

CHAPTER

SIX

Pauline likened the evening to a "road to Emmaus"
experience. Fortunately, she had no idea where that
road ended up.

Beth Stilton's Diary

We finished the book club with the consensus that we loved the book and wished he hadn't killed Nicole but that it was probably best for the story. After selecting our next month's book, *The Kite Runner*, an oldie that somehow we'd all missed, we retired to the kitchen for more wine and Pauline's coffee cake.

I was still feeling frustrated about the general skepticism over my date with Lee. I didn't care what Maxine thought, no one did, but I was worried about the other ladies. I didn't speak much, and this was, by far, not only the most I'd spoken, but the most outlandish thing I'd ever said. I wondered if they thought I had just fantasized the whole thing and thereby lost all credibility. I wished I had kept my mouth shut. I would have if Maxine hadn't called him a sellout. Those were fighting words.

I was drinking my third glass of wine when the doorbell rang. Appropriately, it was the jaunty chorus from "Jingle Bells."

"I hope someone didn't get the wrong time," Pauline said, walking off to answer the door.

"It always happens around the holidays," Shelley said. "They pretend that they got the time wrong when they really just came for the wine."

"Has anyone heard from Cheryl lately?" Kim asked. "She's missed the last two meetings."

"She used to never miss," Deborah said.

"I've spoken to her," Barbara said. "Her father's on hospice in Jacksonville, so she won't be back for a while."

"I'm glad you knew that," Deborah said. "I'll reach out."

"I'll include her in our prayer circle," Kim said.

Just then Pauline said, "Ladies. You'll never believe who decided to visit our humble book club."

The women were speechless at the sight of our visitor. Standing next to Pauline was Lee. Once the initial surprise wore off, Maxine was the first to speak. "Mr. Harper. I'm your biggest fan."

I was seriously tempted to throw my wine in her face. Lee said politely, "Thank you." He looked at me and smiled. He held up a copy of his book. "Beth, you left your book in the limo. I thought you might need it for tonight."

"Thank you." I walked over to him. He hugged me, whispering in my ear, "Are you surprised?"

"Of course not. Why would I be surprised?" I said back. I handed the book to Pauline. "This is for you. Thank you for letting us use your lovely home."

"Why, thank you." She opened the book and read the inscription aloud. She smiled brightly. "Simply delightful." She turned to Lee. "Thank you, dear man."

"My pleasure."

"Would you stay and have some cake and wine?"

"I would love to. Let me inform my driver."

"I'll walk out with you," I said. We walked together out

the front door. Once the door had shut behind us, I said to him, "I did not expect that." My breath clouded in front of me.

He smiled. "Just a moment." He walked to an old Toyota idling in the driveway. He said something to the driver, then came back.

"You took an Uber here?" I said.

He glanced back at the car, then said, "Yeah, it's better this way. Otherwise, Carlie would have been involved."

"I wondered if your shadow was out here waiting for you."

He grinned. "My shadow. That's appropriate."

"This is like the president sneaking out of the White House without the Secret Service."

"Yet, not quite the national security risk."

"No." I looked into his eyes. "But you came."

"I felt bad that you left your book."

"That's the only reason you came?"

"No. That's my excuse for coming. I really just wanted to see you again."

A large smile commandeered my face. I shook my head. "You didn't need an excuse. I wanted to see you too." I looked down a moment, then said, "Last night was basically the greatest night of my life. And the saddest."

"The saddest?"

"What do you do when the best night of your life has come and gone?"

"You do it again."

"I didn't think that was an option. I never thought I'd see you again."

He looked surprised. "Really?"

I nodded. "How did you find me here?"

"Your book club has a website. You told me."

"Right."

"We should probably go back in before the ladies start talking."

"Oh, they already are. Especially your biggest fan."

"I thought you were my biggest fan."

"Apparently not." We walked back into the house. When we got to the kitchen, the talking abruptly stopped. Lee winked at me.

"The two of you met at the book signing?" Shelley asked.

"Actually, we met getting coffee," Lee said.

"I need to drink more coffee," Maxine said.

"So what did you think of my new book?"

"It was fantastic as usual," Maxine said. "But then, no surprise. We're all fans. It was less a review than a celebration."

He cocked his head. "A celebration. I like that."

"Most definitely."

I think all the women were as appalled by Maxine's unctuousness as I was. Then Kim said, "We did have one question. Did you plan on Nicole dying in the end?"

"That seems to be the big question I'm getting. I didn't. But like I told Beth, writing stories is like falling in love—you think you're pulling the strings until you discover you're really the puppet."

"You talk like a poet," Pauline said, swooning. "Now everyone, let's show proper hospitality and let Mr. Harper enjoy himself." She turned back to him. "Did you try my coffee cake?"

"Not yet."

"I'll get you a piece."

"Would you like some wine?" I asked. "Bordeaux of course."

"I'd love some."

As I walked to the counter, Shelley grabbed the bottle to pour a glass for him. She said softly to me, "Well done, dear. He's clearly enamored with you."

"You think?"

"Trust me. This old bird knows enamored."

I smiled and took the glass over to Lee, who was already eating some of Pauline's cake. "Here you are, darling."

"Thank you." He turned to Pauline, who was hovering close to him. "This coffee cake should be classified as a Schedule 1 drug. It's incredibly addicting."

"It was my great-grandmother's recipe. She was a chef at the Drake in Chicago."

"I didn't know I was among royalty," he said.

Pauline beamed.

"How long are you in town?" Shelley asked.

I wondered that myself.

"I leave in the morning for New York. I'm on the *Today* show Monday morning."

"That's exciting," Alice said, showing remarkable courage. "It is, isn't it?"

Lee turned to her, likely noticing her for the first time. "Like most things, it was more exciting the first time, but I still enjoy it. What's your name?"

"It's Alice."

He took her hand. "It's a pleasure to meet you, Alice. And that was a remarkably insightful question."

I saw something in Alice's eyes that I'd never seen, and a large smile crossed her delicate lips. I didn't feel jealous; I felt proud of him. It was as if he took all the love given him by the world and pushed it back out. I didn't think Alice would ever be the same.

"I've done the book circuit," Maxine said, hungry for the attention he was giving Alice. "It's excruciating."

Lee turned and looked at her. His expression remained respectful, but I caught the glimmer of amusement in his eyes. "It really can be. You're a writer too?"

"I dabble," she said with mock humility. "One of my books hit 'the list.'"

The *list*, I thought. The "list" she hit was the local one in the *Lancaster Journal*. I poured Lee another glass of wine, which he immediately drank from. Neither of us rolled our eyes, but I'm certain he wanted to. Or maybe I just did for both of us. He furtively smiled at me, then asked Maxine, "You hit the *New York Times* bestseller list?"

Maxine froze, caught between the truth and the falsehood she had just tried to peddle. "It did well. But reviewers can be a nightmare."

"They can," Lee said. "But they keep us honest."

"They sure do. I'm going to get some more wine," Maxine said, running from the conversation.

"Do you know what time you'll be on the television Monday?" Pauline asked.

"No. I won't know until Sunday evening."

"You know we'll all be watching."

Shelley, bless her soul, said, "So why are you still here? If this is your last night in town, you should not be wasting it with a bunch of fans. You two take off. We're just so honored that you would grace our little book club with your presence. Mr. Harper, you have permanently ensconced yourself in our book club history. None of us will ever forget the evening that J. D. Harper stopped by the Bordeaux Babes Book Club."

"Nor will I," he said. I believed him.

She held up her glass. "Ladies, a toast to Mr. J. D. Harper."

He drained the rest of his wineglass. "Thank you for your hospitality."

"Would you like to take some of my cake back to the hotel with you?" Pauline asked.

"Do I look like the kind of fool who would turn that down?"

Pauline laughed. "You're just darling. Let me get you a Tupperware." She cut off a large piece of cake, put it in a Tupperware bowl, and handed it to him. "Don't worry about returning the container, dear. I've got plenty."

"Thank you. And if you find someone eating coffee cake in my next book, you'll know it was inspired by you."

Pauline looked like she might faint with excitement.

"Good night, everyone," I said.

Lee took the Tupperware in one hand and mine in the other. "It's been a pleasure. Thank you."

He helped me into my coat, then we walked out of the house.

"Thank you for enduring that."

"It was fun. Thank you for inviting me."

"Did I?"

"You did. I just wasn't very receptive to your invitation."

"Now where are we going?"

"Dinner," he said. "Is there any good barbeque around here? I haven't eaten since lunch."

"We have Coachman's. It's not fancy, but it's kind of a local landmark."

"Let's do it."

"Should I drive?"

"Let's let the kid drive. Are you okay leaving your car?"

"We can come back for it. If it's not too much trouble."

"It's not."

We got in the Uber. After shutting his door, Lee leaned forward to the driver. "Do you know Coachman's barbecue?"

"The one on Gravel Pit Road?"

"Is there more than one Coachman's?"

"Not that I know of."

"Then that must be the one. Take us there, please."

"Yes, sir. I love their chicken. I might get something to eat myself."

Lee sat back next to me. "Where were we?"

"I was just about to apologize. The ladies avalanched you. I've never seen them so excited."

"Avalanched. That's a good word. They were lovely."

"You were lovely with them. Even Maxine."

"Maxine. She's the author."

"Yes. And sycophant."

He grinned. "She needed the attention the most. Everyone wants to feel important. The lucky ones can get it from inside. The others look outside of themselves. Maxine is empty inside."

"That's exactly who she is." I thought about his words, then asked, "Which are you, an inside or outside looker?"

His forehead creased. "Good question. It's hard to know anymore. I'm so surrounded by approbation, I'm not sure how I am without it. Fame's a two-edged sword. Some become more affected by it and need more and more; others become satiated and start longing for anonymity. Honestly, I've seen both."

"Well, you made them all feel important."

"I hope so. Tell me about Alice."

"I don't know her well. She's very quiet."

"Is she married?"

I suddenly felt a twinge of jealousy. I had seen the way he looked into her eyes.

"Are you interested in her?"

He looked at me with amused incredulity. "No."

"I don't think she's married. I think she was, but they're divorced."

"She was abused, wasn't she?" he said. "Like you."

"Her friend who brought her to the club told us she was." I looked at him in wonder. "How did you know that?"

"I pay attention."

Coachman's was as much an institution as a restaurant. It had been around for nearly half a century and had miniature golf, an outdoor pavilion, and a party room. Even though it was late, there were still people in line waiting to order.

Lee ordered the meatloaf with mashed potatoes, while I had a small cheesesteak sandwich. We skipped dessert since we'd already had Pauline's coffee cake and had more in the car.

"This is pretty good," Lee said.

"I picture you eating at five-star restaurants, champagne and caviar. Not meatloaf and mashed potatoes."

"I'm a comfort-food kind of guy. Meatloaf, mashed potatoes and gravy, food doesn't get much better. Especially in the South. I love southern cooking."

"I thought you were leaving town today."

"No, I just had something personal. I'd tell you what it is, but you'd probably mock me."

"I might. Try me."

"The reason I came to Lancaster this tour is because there's a big Civil War antiques show going on."

"You mean, those pewter soldiers you collect."

He nodded. "You know you have pretty eyes."

"That was a clever deflection. Thank you. So do you." I shook my head. "This still seems like a dream."

"I could pinch you."

"Later," I said. "I wonder how many people in here read your books."

He shrugged.

"Do people stop you everywhere for autographs?"

"That depends on where I am. One of the Chicago media escorts told me that Grisham can walk through a suburban mall, and no one will recognize him, but if he walks into an airport he's mobbed. It's about context. Since the last movie and the press junket, things have gotten worse; now everyone wants photographs so they can post them on their social media."

As if I had manifested it, at that very moment a young woman stopped at our table. "Excuse me, sir, but are you J. D. Harper?"

He glanced over at me. I raised my eyebrows.

"Yes, I am," he said to her.

"I knew it." She turned to a table filled with other twenty-something women. "I told you it's him." She looked back. "I'm such a huge fan. Could I possibly get a picture with you?"

"Sure."

He stood up.

"I can take it," I said.

"Thank you, but I like selfies," she said, not even looking at me. She lifted the camera and nestled into Lee, her mouth opening in a big, toothy grin. "Smile."

Lee also smiled. I noticed that nearly everyone in the restaurant was watching. Someone in a booth across from us was videoing them.

She snapped at least a dozen photos, then lowered her phone. "Thank you."

"You're welcome."

Then she said, "We all think you're really hot."

"Thank you."

As she was leaving him, two other young women from her table walked up, then someone from another table.

"I think we need to go," I said. I stood and took his arm. "I'm sorry, I've got to get Mr. Harper to his next appointment. Thanks for reading."

"I'm sorry," he said, waving to the growing crowd as I dragged him out of the restaurant. The temperature had dropped still more, and the winter air felt like a brisk slap. Luckily our driver was in the car, otherwise our departure would have been awkward. Lee opened the door for me. I slid across the seat to the other side. There were still people looking out the window at us. Our driver had a Coachman's sack in his lap.

"You're good at that," Lee said to me.

"That was getting out of control."

"Welcome back," our driver said, wiping his fingers on a napkin. "Where to now?"

"Back to where we picked this young lady up, then to the Lancaster Marriott at Penn Square."

"I can drive you to your hotel," I said.

"Thank you. I'd like that." He reached over and took my hand.

As the Uber driver pulled up to my car, he said, "Mr. Harper, I googled you while you were inside. I'm not much of a reader, but my mom's a big fan. She freaked out when I told her I was driving you. Could I get a picture of us?"

"Sure."

It was really a video. "Look who I'm with, Mom. Mr. Harper, would you give her a shout-out, her name is Sandra."

"Hi, Sandra," Lee said. "Your son is a relatively safe driver, though he texts at intersections, and he doesn't know the difference between a photo and a video."

The driver laughed. "Cool, man. Take it easy."

As late as it was, Maxine's car was still parked at the curb. I half expected her to spring from the Honda and ambush us.

"Party still going on?" Lee asked, his hands in his coat pockets.

"That's Maxine's car. She's still here."

"My biggest fan?"

"That's the one."

We walked to my Volkswagen and got in. The vinyl seats creaked from the cold. After sitting down, I looked over. He was just looking at me. He looked beautiful.

"How are you?" he asked.

"I'm happy."

"Good. So am I."

"You must be exhausted."

"I was exhausted before I started the tour."

"I'm not helping by keeping you up late." I started the car. "You're staying at the Marriott?"

"I'm not in a hurry," he said. "Let's talk."

I shut off the car. "I was hoping you would say that."

"You might want to keep the car going, though. For the heater."

"Sorry." I started the car back up, then turned the heater on full.

"Where do you live?" he asked.

"Not too far from here. I rent a house from my best friend. Her name is Frankie. We used to be roommates, then she got married a few years ago and I just took on the rental. It's a nice place. Would you like to see it?" I was talking too much. I do that when I'm nervous.

"Maybe next time."

"Sorry. I'm acting nervous."

He looked perplexed. "Why?"

"Really? I'm alone here with you. I still can't believe this is happening. Things like this don't happen to me. And after you left yesterday, I realized you never answered my question."

"Which one?"

"Why you chose me?"

He suddenly looked thoughtful. "I suppose that I was still trying to answer that question to myself. Sometimes we connect with someone, and we don't know why. I obviously found you attractive, but that's just surface. What I'm feeling isn't surface.

"It began at the coffee shop when you started talking about your life and how *Bethel* impacted you. I didn't just feel your vulnerability, I felt an emotional connection, like we're two broken people and the jagged edges fit together. Like a puzzle."

"Are you broken?"

"More than you know."

"You have no idea how hard it was for me to come to the signing. You were the first hope I've felt in men for decades. What if you were nothing like your books, and I had another experience like I had with my father?"

He looked at me soulfully but said nothing.

"I've thought about what you said about me looking for my father, that I was looking for home, you were right. When you held me last night." I paused to control my emotions. "For the first time in my life, I felt like I was home."

We both let the words settle in the silence of the night.

Then he reached over and took my hand. "What is home to you?"

"Home is someplace safe and warm, where people care for each other. Maybe it's the fiction I want to believe exists somewhere."

"Bethel," he said softly. "How far is your house from here?"

"About ten minutes."

"I've changed my mind. We should go there. I really want to hold you, and this console is in the way."

I put my seat belt on. "I bet I can make it in seven."

CHAPTER

SEVEN

It's my experience that more church fellowship takes place in a church's lobby than its chapel.

Beth Stilton's Diary

It was four in the morning when I got back from dropping Lee off at his hotel after what was undoubtedly the best night of my life. I don't know what compelled me to go to church after only three and a half hours of sleep. Maybe I was feeling particularly blessed. Or, more likely, I was hoping to run into the book club ladies. I felt like we were bound together as a group of witnesses to a shared miracle.

Church didn't disappoint. Ironically, the sermon was on miracles. And on the way out I ran into Pauline, Kim, and Deborah in the church lobby.

"That was quite a delightful surprise you had for us," Pauline said.

"It was a surprise for me too," I said. "I didn't expect that."

"How did the two of you meet?" Deborah asked.

"It was happenstance. While I was waiting for the book signing to begin, I went to get a coffee. When they announced my coffee, Lee and I both went for it. We ended up sharing a table together to drink."

"Happenstance my foot," Pauline said. "It was fate."

"I loved posting about it," Deborah said. "All my friends think I'm a celebrity. I'm surprised at how many of my friends are closet Harper fans. I think we're going to get an influx of new club members."

"What did you do after you left?" Kim asked.

"We went to Coachman's. He hadn't had dinner."

"Coachman's? The chicken place? You couldn't have gone someplace swankier?"

"That's where he wanted to go. He wanted comfort food."

"He sounds like a real down-to-earth man," Pauline said.

"He is, but nothing else about this feels real."

Deborah said, "You should have seen Maxine after you left. She drank her entire bottle of wine, then half of mine."

"And a quarter of mine," Kim added.

"She was three sheets to the wind," Deborah said. "Tabitha had to give her a ride home."

"I wondered why her car was still there when we got back."

"Are you excited to see your man on TV tomorrow?"

"Of course. I've set my DVR too so I can watch it over and over."

"We'll also be watching," Pauline said.

They started to leave, when Kim said, "Beth."

"Yes?"

"Trust me on this. Don't overthink it. Just enjoy it. You deserve this."

I hugged her. "Thank you."

It was maybe the greatest advice anyone had ever given me. Of course I didn't follow it.

CHAPTER

EIGHT

*The good news is that everyone loves him. I suppose,
in a way, that's the bad news as well.*

Beth Stilton's Diary

I woke the next morning like it was Christmas. At least Christmas for a normal childhood. I rolled over and checked the clock. It was a quarter to seven. The *Today* show began at seven. I turned on the television set, sound turned up loud, then made myself a coffee. At eight thirty, just before going to a commercial break, they showed a picture of Lee's book and announced that he would be on the next segment:

"He's one of America's most popular authors. His new book has reviewers raving and his fans' hearts palpitating. Join us in the next segment with J. D. Harper. We'll be right back."

The show returned from the break with a quick zoom-in on Lee and two of the hosts, the three of them sitting on tall stools. Lee was wearing a loose-fitting silver Armani suit with a black turtleneck. He looked like a movie star. It was surreal seeing this man I'd spent alone time with on display for millions.

He handled himself well, professional and charming, which likely wasn't difficult considering how fawning the two female hosts were. They treated him like Brad Pitt meets Ernest Hemingway, and one of them was shamelessly flirting. I was uncomfortable, a feeling that, when I homed in on it, I recognized as jealousy.

As soon as the segment ended, I immediately began getting congratulatory texts from the women in the book club. It was the first time I'd received that kind of attention from the club. Maybe from any group. The truth was, they weren't the texts I wanted. I kept hoping I'd hear from him. I think I was hoping for a little validation that he hadn't already forgotten me.

The text never came.

After watching that segment, the reality that he was way out of my league couldn't have been starker. I had to accept the likely fact that he probably had, to borrow an old nautical reference, a woman in every port.

Truthfully, despite the obvious pain of jealousy, worse things could happen. The short time we spent together was easily the highlight of my year—a rare day of sunshine in a very long season of overcast weather.

The problem was, I might have been one of many to him, but he was the only man I had remotely let into my life for years. And he wasn't one I could likely forget.

Except for two telemarketers, my phone was quiet the rest of the day. Finally, I turned it off and went to bed. "So it goes."

CHAPTER

NINE

He wants me to meet him in New York. I really have no idea why he's so interested in me. Maybe he needs a kidney donor.

Beth Stilton's Diary

I woke sad. Back to my normal dull life. I got out of bed, made my coffee, and was about to get in the shower when I remembered that I hadn't turned my phone on. I'll admit that there was still some hope that there might be a text from Lee, but I forced myself to push it away. Yesterday had been a day of minute-to-minute heartbreak. I didn't want to start my day the way it had ended. Then my phone started vibrating. Three text messages popped up on my phone.

Sorry it's so late. It's Lee. You there?

Hello? Anybody there?

It's morning. Wake up already.

I smiled. He hadn't forgotten me. Then I saw that I had two voicemail messages. I was about to listen to the first one, when my phone rang. It was him. I took a deep breath. *Don't sound too eager.*

"Good morning, rock star," I said.

"Oh, good. You answered. I was about to call your neighbors to have them do a welfare check on you."

"You don't know my neighbors."

"I know. It was hyperbole. How are you?"

"I'm good. Better now that you called."

90

"Sorry I didn't call you yesterday, my day was nonstop. By the time I got back to the hotel it was past midnight."

"You're an important guy."

"That's what they tell me," he said. "Did you watch my segment?"

"Of course I did."

"How did I do?"

"You were handsome, well-spoken, charismatic . . ."

"But did I make people want to read the book?"

"If I wasn't already a fan, I'd be one now."

"That's what I wanted to hear," he said. "What are you doing?"

"I was just about to get in the shower. Then work."

"Well, I'm suddenly feeling a little awkward, so I'll just say it. I know we just met, but I miss you."

There was a long pause. I wasn't sure if he was going to say more, or if it was my turn.

"Are you still there?" he asked.

"Yes. I'm here. I was . . ." I sighed. "Since we're being honest, I spent the whole day hoping you'd call and afraid that you had already forgotten me."

"I'm sorry I didn't call right away."

"No, this is wonderful. I'm so glad you called."

"So am I. I'm in New York for three more days. I have more media today and a book signing in Long Island tonight, then tomorrow I have meetings with my publisher. They're celebrating the book release with a champagne toast. Would you like to join me?"

"In New York?"

"I doubt I could convince the whole publishing house to come to Lancaster, so if that's okay, I can send a car. It's faster than flying. Have you been to New York?"

"When I was a teenager. When do you want me to come?"

"When can you come?"

I had a very short battle between desire and not acting too eager. Desire won. "Anytime."

"How about I send a car to pick you up tomorrow morning at nine? That way we can meet for lunch."

"What should I wear?"

"Business casual. And I'll need your address for the car service."

"I'll text it."

"Then I'll see you soon."

"Wait, how long will I be there?"

"That depends on how long you want to stay."

"How long are you in New York?"

"I'll be here until Friday afternoon, then I'm headed to my house in the Cape for Thanksgiving."

"Then I'll leave when you do."

"It's up to you," he said. "But bring some extra clothes just in case."

"Okay," I said. "Thank you for calling."

"Thank you for answering. Ciao."

We hung up. *In case of what?*

CHAPTER

TEN

I met Lee's agent. She's not what I expected, but, considering my author, she should have been.

Beth Stilton's Diary

I was up early the next morning, legs shaved, makeup on, packed. I was still mulling over the meaning of his *just in case*, so I brought extra clothes, including a swimsuit and workout clothes. I was near the front window when the car, a shiny black Lincoln Nautilus, pulled up at five minutes before the hour. The driver, an older, tall thin man wearing a black jacket and cap, walked up to my door. I opened before he rang the bell.

"Ms. Stilton, I'm your driver, Carl. Are you ready?"

"Yes, sir."

He smiled. "Call me Carl. Do you have any luggage I could assist with?"

"Just this."

He grabbed my bag's handle. "I'll take that."

"I still need to make sure everything's off inside. I'll be right out."

I ran back in, lowered the thermostat, checked each room, then came back out. I locked my front door, then walked down to the car. Carl opened the back door for me as I approached.

"Thank you."

"My pleasure, ma'am."

I had never had a "car" with a uniformed driver pull up at my house. Even though I didn't know my neighbors well,

I kind of hoped someone was watching. I wanted someone besides just me to witness this moment.

A half hour after we'd left my house Lee called.

"You're on your way?"

"I am. The car was right on time."

"We're having lunch at Jupiter with my agent at twelve thirty. The driver knows the address. I'll see you there."

That gave me about 160 miles to remember how to act like a normal person.

The car stopped in front of Rockefeller Center. Even though it was daytime, the giant, iconic Christmas tree above the gold statue of Prometheus was lit up, and the plaza was packed with people, both locals and tourists.

"Let me tell you where you're going," Carl said. "You see that little booth right there? That's an elevator. You take it down to concourse level. There's a mall under this entire area. Just follow the rink around, you'll come to a restaurant called Jupiter. That's where Mr. Harper and his guest will be waiting. If you get lost, there are kiosks around or ask anyone. Unless they're a tourist, they'll know." He handed me a card. "Or call me. I'll be happy to help."

I took out my purse. "You do take credit cards?"

Carl smiled. "That's been taken care of, ma'am."

"And the tip?"

"That's been taken care of too. You enjoy your time in New York."

The restaurant was easy to find. Lee greeted me as I

walked into the restaurant. He hugged me, then led me back to a table to meet his agent.

"Laurie, this is Beth. Beth, this is my agent, Laurie."

Lee's agent wasn't what I expected. I thought he'd be a tall, slick-looking gentleman in an expensive Italian suit. Instead, *she* was a pleasant-looking woman, short, with stylish granny glasses and curly silver hair.

"It's a pleasure to meet you," she said, extending her hand to shake. "Lee has talked so much about you."

He raised one eyebrow. "Not *so* much."

"*Incessantly*," she said. "How was the drive in?"

"It was nice. It was a nice car."

"Let's sit down," Lee said. "I'm famished."

"It's too early in the day to be famished," Laurie said.

"I took the liberty of ordering some appetizers and wine. And here's your menu."

I looked over the fare. "What's this *Alfabeto in brodo*?"

"Alphabet soup," Lee said.

"I'll have that."

"I like her," Laurie said to Lee.

I smiled. "I like you too. How are the meetings with your publisher going?"

"Well," Lee said.

"For him they are," Laurie said. "I'm not talking to them. We're negotiating his next contract. It always gets ugly now."

"She's in pit bull mode," Lee said.

"I'm always in pit bull mode."

"Lee shook his head. She wants you to believe that, but she's not. She's really a sheep in wolf's clothing."

"Don't call me a sheep."

"What about a wolf?"

"That's okay."

I loved their relationship.

"Did you see Lee on the *Today* show?" Laurie asked.

"I did. He was great."

"He *was* great. He's a natural at promotion."

"It's my background in public relations," Lee said.

"It's your cute baby face," Laurie said. "And brilliant blue eyes."

"How is the book doing?" I asked.

"Dailies are up," Laurie said. (I didn't know what that meant.) "Looking at the field, he should debut at number one, but I never say that out loud. I don't want to jinx it. And lists can be . . . unreliable."

I suddenly panicked. "I left my suitcase in the car."

"You didn't," Lee said. "I asked the driver to take it to the hotel. It will be waiting for you when you get there."

I sighed in relief. "Thank you. You think of everything."

"No, I just don't forget a bad experience. The first time I came here I was lugging a massive suitcase with me through the sidewalks of New York. No one liked that."

"It was awkward," Laurie said. "Very awkward."

"I was awkward," Lee said.

"Very, very awkward," Laurie said.

The meal was lovely. For dessert we had olive oil cake. We

walked into the underground mall and took the elevator back up to the street. The cold air braced us as the door opened.

"I'm headed back to the office," Laurie said. "You're meeting with your editor?"

"Yes, then marketing. I'll just meet you at the toast."

"I'll see you there." She turned to me. "It's a pleasure meeting you, Beth. Be nice to him. He's a good guy."

"I know he is. And it's a pleasure to meet you."

"I'll see you tonight." She turned and walked toward the street, holding her hand up for a taxi.

"Do you like her?" Lee asked.

"Yes. Very much."

"Good. We're very close friends. She's been great. She's my guide through the publishing jungle."

"How long have you been together?"

"The whole way. She was a junior agent when I found her. I was calling literary agencies, and she answered the phone. We had a good talk about the book, and she asked me to email her the manuscript. She called the next day, said it might be the best book she had ever read, but, because of her situation, she would have to pass her recommendation on to her boss, the agent she was being mentored by. He wasn't interested and told her that if she wanted to pursue me, have at it. And she did."

"That book was *Bethel*?"

He nodded. "Yes, it was."

"I bet that other agent regrets that."

"I'm sure he does too. Because he lost not just a ton of money, but also the clout that comes with having a brand-name author. Everyone wants J. D. Harper's agent. Laurie deserves it. She's smart, tough, but surprisingly pleasant." He smiled. "She has a place up on Cape Cod near mine. Her partner just bought her a boat, so she fancies herself a sea captain now. I'm getting her one of those little captain hats for Christmas."

"Yours is such a different world from mine," I said.

"Just remember, it's not what I grew up with either. And you have me."

I loved that he said that.

"I have a meeting with my editor for the next hour, then we're recording some marketing promos. I thought you might like to rest after that ride in. I have you booked in a junior suite at the Mark hotel. They have a very nice spa, and I made a four o'clock reservation for a massage for you. Everything is taken care of.

"I'll be by to get you at six thirty. We'll take a cab to the publisher. The toast is at seven and we have dinner reservations at Keens Steakhouse at eight thirty. If you're hungry before then, you can order something from room service."

"Where are you staying?"

"I'm in the room next to yours." He reached into his wallet and handed me a credit card. "Just use this if you need anything. The hotel and amenities are already on my card, so you shouldn't need it. Just don't go crazy on Fifth Avenue."

"I'll be good."

A cab pulled up to the curb in front of us.

"Here you go."

"Oh, what's the address?"

"He'll know." He opened the door for me, then said to the driver, "Take her to the Mark on Madison."

The driver grumbled something that sounded vaguely affirmative, then put the car in gear. Lee waved to me as we drove off.

It all felt like a dream. I tried to forget that my dreams were usually nightmares.

CHAPTER

ELEVEN

*Tonight, the publisher held a champagne toast for
Lee and the success of his new book. Lee made me
feel as if the evening was as much a celebration of
me as it was of him.*

Beth Stilton's Diary

I had looked up the Mark on the way to the hotel. It was called one of the world's most exquisite hotels, and I could see why. The lobby was gorgeous, and the staff were nice, not pretentious. My bag was waiting, as I hoped, and they reminded me about my massage appointment.

My room was on the third floor and was more luxurious than anything I had ever experienced. The bathroom had a soaking tub made of marble with polished nickel fittings. There was even a heated towel rack.

I filled the tub up, poured in the bath oils, then lay back and closed my eyes. I could get used to this.

I went down for my massage as well, and by the time I got back, I was so relaxed my bones felt like rubber. I lay on the bed and watched television for a half hour, then got ready for the toast. I wanted to look especially nice for him.

Lee knocked on my door at six thirty. While I was ultra relaxed, he looked frazzled.

"Hi," he said with a weary smile. "You look lovely."

"So do you. But you look tired. You didn't get to rest, did you?"

He shook his head. "I didn't even get to my room. When I'm in town everyone at the publisher's wants a piece of me."

"That's good, though. Right?"

He thought a moment. "It's better than the alternative. Should we go?"

"Yes."

We took a cab to the publisher's building on Avenue of the Americas. We passed security and took the elevator to the twenty-first-floor penthouse. The staff and guests were scattered around the room talking. Laurie was already there. Carlie, whom I had surprisingly forgotten about, was also there. She immediately moved to Lee's side.

The president of the publishing house greeted us, shaking Lee's hand first. "This is your party," he said. "We're here to celebrate you. Again."

"Thank you, Jonathan."

"We're glad you're here too, Beth," he said to me. I was surprised that he knew my name. While Lee talked to some of the other guests, I approached Carlie.

Before I could speak she said, "It's good to see you, Beth."

"Have you been in New York the whole time?" I asked.

"The whole time?" she said. "What do you mean?"

"I mean, since Lee got here."

"I go everywhere Lee goes," she said. "That's my job. I take care of him."

I wasn't sure how to take her tone. "You do a good job of it."

She didn't say anything but stepped back.

Laurie was watching the exchange and stepped forward. "Hi, Beth, it's good to see you so soon."

"Likewise."

"Hello, dear Carlie."

Carlie's voice rose to a friendlier pitch. "Hi, Laurie."

Laurie leaned into me. "Don't worry about it. She's a great

assistant, but she's as territorial as a hippopotamus. I've had to put her in her place a few times myself."

"Are hippos territorial?"

"Oh yeah. They're the worst."

I wondered how she knew this.

The president walked over to a table crowded with plastic champagne flutes arranged around an oversized bottle of Moët & Chandon.

"All right, everyone come take your drinks."

I picked up a flute and stood next to Laurie.

"It looks like you are all ready," Jonathan said. "I'm not officially supposed to know this, so no one is to post this yet, but my mole inside the *New York Times* has informed me that we have yet another number one *New York Times* bestseller. Congratulations, Lee. We are enormously proud to be your publisher." He lifted his glass. "To J. D. Harper and *Winter in Arcadia*. May it be just another footnote in a very long and successful career."

Everyone touched glasses. Lee turned to me and held out his glass.

"I'm proud of you," I said. "I hope this is still exciting."

"Thank you. It's exciting that you're here to share it." He lifted his glass. "Cheers."

"Cheers," I said.

"We would be delighted to hear from you," Jonathan said to Lee. "If you would oblige us."

"My pleasure." He walked to the front of the room. "It's truly a pleasure working with you all," Lee said. "Thank you all for all your hard work. It takes a big team to create, distribute, and sell a book. I've got the Chicago Bulls of teams. And by that, I mean during their Michael Jordan years."

"Go Knicks," someone said.

"Go Knicks," Lee said back. "And go us. We've got a lot more books to sell, and I will be on the road for another thirteen cities before the new year. So I wish you all a very happy Thanksgiving, a Merry Christmas, and a happy and successful new year."

Everyone lifted their glasses again and drank.

CHAPTER

TWELVE

*People often say that they would have liked to have
been a fly on the wall, forgetting that that's where
flies usually meet their demise.*

Beth Stilton's Diary

By seven thirty most of the celebratory group had left the penthouse, except for a small circle of editors engaged in a serious discussion.

Lee, Jonathan, Laurie, Carlie, and I took cabs over to one of Lee's favorite restaurants, Keens Steakhouse on Thirty-Sixth Street. Keens, Lee told me, was a New York institution and was once a members-only pipe club. Their roster included nearly one hundred thousand names, from authors, actors, and playwrights to politicians and sports heroes, including Teddy Roosevelt, Babe Ruth, Albert Einstein, General Douglas MacArthur, and Buffalo Bill Cody.

The crowded restaurant had a pub-like feel, with a large, painted nude hanging above the bar like an old western saloon. We were taken up a short flight of stairs and seated in the Bull Moose Room, a cozier, dark-paneled room that had a large moose head mounted above the fireplace and a framed invitation to Teddy Roosevelt's inauguration as well as other Roosevelt artifacts.

"I don't come here enough," Jonathan announced as we sat down. "I've never had a bad meal at Keens. Of course that's probably because I order the same thing every time."

"The mutton," Lee said.

"Yes, their specialty." He said to me, "You will notice the clay pipes overhead. It was an old English tradition. The men would leave their pipes at an establishment, as they were fragile and often broke in their saddlebags. This was a men's smoking club, and women were prohibited until 1905, when Lillie Langtry, the famous actress and paramour of England's King Edward, sued Keens for being denied access. She won her case, and it's said she wore her feathered boa inside to order their famous mutton."

"It sounds like I should have the mutton," I said.

"Women fought for that right," he replied.

"Thank you." I whispered to Lee, "What if I don't like mutton?"

"I've got you," he said.

Even though I knew I wasn't paying, the price was still as breathtaking as the club's history. Lee and I decided to share the Chateaubriand steak for two, an iceberg lettuce wedge with blue cheese dressing and bacon and carrots with brown butter. Since they were most famous for their massively large muttonchop, we also ordered a "taste of mutton" so I could, at least, say that I had tried it and pay homage to Ms. Langtry and her battle for equal rights to fine mutton. All the talk of history and celebrity just further confirmed to me how out of place I really was.

After we were eating, Jonathan said to me, "Your last name is Stilton," he said. "Like the cheese."

"Just like the cheese," I said.

"We've got some really great cheese restaurants in New York."

"I didn't know that cheese restaurants were a thing."

"They are. Though I shouldn't assume you like cheese

just because of your last name. After all, my mother's maiden name was Payne."

I smiled at the inference. "I like cheese," I said. "Especially Stilton."

"You probably know that it's illegal to make Stilton cheese in Stilton."

"Yes. I knew that."

"It's the lawyers' doing."

"And the agents," Laurie said. "The fly in the ointment."

"We love our agents," Jonathan said.

"Sure you do," she said.

He diplomatically added, "Just sometimes more than others."

Lee smiled at the exchange, but he was quieter than he had been. He'd been exhausted before we left for the toast. I wondered how he was keeping his eyes open.

Carlie sat quietly at one corner of the table, watching us. I wondered what was going through her mind.

Jonathan said to Lee, "Laurie says you're headed back to the Cape for Thanksgiving."

"Yes, then back out on the road."

"Are you having a big gathering?"

"No. Just my brother. Maybe a few friends." He glanced over at me. "Carlie's going home to Michigan. And Laurie is going to . . ." He turned to Laurie.

"Laurie," Laurie said, speaking in third person, "is going to Orlando to be abused by her aunt. Three days of her telling me what an *Umglik* I am and asking, in front of Julie, why I don't find a nice Jewish boy and have *kinder*."

"How about you, Beth?" Laurie asked.

"The usual," I said.

"With the family?"

"Yes," I said, "the whole family." Lee glanced at me. He knew there was no family.

"I feel like I just ate Thanksgiving dinner," Lee said. "I don't think I have room for dessert."

"We shall see," Jonathan said. He ordered three desserts for the table: a banana foster, crème brûlée, and an affogato. It all got eaten by everyone except Lee, who had a decaf coffee while I ate too much of the banana foster. I don't know if anyone else noticed, but he was struggling to stay awake.

"We need to get you to bed," I said.

"That's a really good idea." He stood. "I don't want to break up the party, but I need to get some sleep. My publicity team has been working me like a rented mule."

"I'm glad they're doing their job," Jonathan said. "But we should wrap things up. Again, congratulations. And a happy Thanksgiving, all."

CHAPTER

THIRTEEN

*In the cocktail party of life, it is my present self's
responsibility to see that my past self and my future
self stay as far apart as possible.*

Beth Stilton's Diary

After dinner, Lee and Carlie spoke for a moment, then Lee and I separated from the group. We walked down Thirty-Sixth, then hailed a cab at the corner. After we were in, I said, "That was probably the best meal I've ever had." I looked at him. "Definitely the best day."

He looked at me for a moment, then he took off his seat belt and slid over next to me. He put his hand around the back of my head and brought me into him. We began to kiss. The city, in all its energy and glory, passed by us unwitnessed. We kissed until we reached the hotel. Lee told me to stay where I was, he paid the driver, then came around the car, took my hand, and helped me out.

This was new territory for me. I had never felt so special or cared for in my entire life. But, as they say, the price of happiness is the risk of losing it, and fear began to seep up in my chest like groundwater. What if he grew bored with me? What if he met some other fan in some other Starbucks, and I stopped hearing from him? I pushed the fear from my mind. This time was worth it, no matter what price I had to pay. Or so I tried to convince myself.

We came out of the elevator and walked down the hallway, stopping between our two rooms. The hall was quiet with no one else around except for a room service waitress who hurried by with a friendly hello. He gently pressed me back against the hallway wall and we kissed more. It was so nice.

"You look so sleepy," I said as we parted. I ran my finger down the bridge of his nose to his lips. "Sleepy and handsome."

"Not too sleepy," he said, almost slurring his words.

"Want to come in and watch a movie?"

"What do you want to watch?"

I grinned. "Does it matter?"

He sighed pleasantly. "I'm going to brush my teeth. I'll be right back."

"I'll leave the door ajar," I said.

He went into his room, and I went into mine. I wished I had brought fancier sleepwear—not that what I had was bad. I had brought a one-piece sleep shirt, which was form-fitting and cute. I slid it on, then went and brushed my teeth. I went back out to the bedroom. I was pulling down the duvet as Lee came to my door.

"Knock," he said.

"Come in."

He stepped inside. He hadn't really changed much, except to lose his jacket, tie, and shoes, roll up his sleeves, and unbutton his top button.

"You look pretty," he said.

"Thank you. You look handsome." I pushed the pillows back against the headboard. "Lie down, please."

He sat on the bed, then lifted his feet up and lay back into the pillows while I turned on the television.

"Let's see what they have." I began scrolling through the

selections, then stopped at a comedy romance. "How about this?" I asked, turning back. His eyes were closed.

"Lee?"

His breathing grew louder and more rhythmic. I walked over to his side of the bed and saw that he was fast asleep.

"Not enough jet fuel," I said softly. I crawled onto the bed next to him. For a moment I just looked into his face. He had such a beautiful face. It was strong and masculine. But even more, it was kind. Two thoughts, born from my life experience, clouded my mind. *How did I end up here? How is this going to end?*

CHAPTER

FOURTEEN

Jungle peanut butter, pine pollen smoothies, caviar and candied walnuts. I'm not in Lancaster anymore.
Beth Stilton's Diary

I was awake when the sun, hidden behind blinds, started to illuminate the room. I didn't want morning to come. I wanted to stay right where I was, warm and safe and loved. It was the first time in years that I'd gone to bed without Ambien or some other sleeping pill. And one of the few nights I hadn't woken screaming.

Lee rolled over and put an arm around me. He was still wearing his dress shirt from the night before.

"Sorry about last night," he said softly, his face just a few inches from mine and his eyes still closed. I loved the warmth of his breath on my face. "I think I fell asleep. Or you roofied me."

"I might have."

"At least you had fun." He opened his eyes. "Do you know what time it is?"

"Today is no clock day."

He lifted an eyebrow. "No clocks?"

"No clocks. I've decided that today will last forever."

He smiled. "This is the perfect beginning of forever. Can I sleep some more?"

"If I can hold you," I said. I pulled his head onto my chest. "You work so hard. Everyone wants something from you."

"What do you want from me?"

"This."

He fell asleep again. I held him.

He slept for nearly an hour more before his eyes opened and looked up at me.

"Morning," I whispered. "Again."

"I think my tour is finally catching up with me."

"You've been on a marathon."

"If this is the finish line, it was worth the run."

I kissed his forehead. "Not the finish line. Just a rest stop."

"How long have you been up?"

"Hours," I said.

"I'm hungry. Are you hungry?"

"Yes. Can we get some breakfast?"

"Of course. Do you want to go out or get room service?"

"Room service, please."

"Will you call them?"

I smiled. "I would if I could get up. You're on me."

"Oh, that." He lifted himself up onto his arms and kissed me, then he swung his legs over the side of the bed. "I feel like I've slept for days."

"Just half of one."

He raked a hand back through his hair, then looked at himself in the wall mirror. He looked like a wrinkled version of what had walked in my room last night. "I slept in this?"

"I hate it when men sleep with their socks on."

He laughed. "But you're okay with slacks? At least you look cute."

"It's not Victoria's Secret, but it's not Kmart."

"Are there still Kmarts?"

"I'm sure there are somewhere. They keep them next to the Blockbusters." I climbed out of bed and walked over to the credenza. "Here's the room service menu. Wait, it's called 'in-room dining.'"

"'In-room dining' sounds fancier."

"It gets better. It's in-room dining straight from Chef Jean-George's kitchen." I continued to read about their restaurant.

"I'll have a bowl of oatmeal, please."

"Oatmeal? This is Chef Jean-Georges. The man has a hyphen in his name. You don't just order oatmeal from someone with a hyphen. It has to be fancy. Like oatmeal brûlée. Or artisanal oatmeal infused with saffron capers."

"Are you always this funny in the morning?"

"No. I usually start my day with a primal scream."

He smiled. "Tell Chef George he can put caviar on my oatmeal if he wants. I'll pick it off."

"It's Chef Jean-Georges, and there is no oatmeal and caviar, but he does have smoothies. Here is a pollen smoothie. It has pine pollen, jungle peanut butter, dates, banana, and almond milk."

"What's jungle peanut butter?"

"I don't know, but it sounds wild. Wait, that's from their vegan restaurant menu. Here's the real breakfast. Omelets, eggs Benedict with roasted potatoes, buttermilk pancakes, French toast with sauteed stone apple, avocado toast . . ."

"Do they have oatmeal?"

"Yes, they have Irish steel-cut oatmeal. It comes with dried sour cherries, steamed milk, and brown sugar, and you can add banana and berries."

"I'll have that. With candied walnuts."

"They don't have candied walnuts."

"It's the Mark. They'll find them."

"Okay, and to drink they have freshly squeezed orange and grapefruit juice and they have La Colombe coffee, including espresso, latte, or cappuccino."

"I'll have an espresso shot, please. And a small grapefruit juice."

"Should I have them add an energy shot to your espresso?"

"No, it already is an energy shot. What are you having?"

"I'm going to have the eggs Benedict with one buttermilk pancake on the side. Do you think they'll let me do that?"

"They'll let you do whatever you want." He stood. "I'm going to go shower quick and I'll be back."

We kissed again, then he walked out. He was back, shaved and dressed, as the in-room waitress was leaving the room.

"Men can get ready so fast," I said.

"It's true."

His oatmeal looked good. And there was a small dish next to it with sour cherries and candied walnuts.

After we'd started eating, Lee said, "I'm sorry about Laurie asking you about Thanksgiving. She didn't know."

"Sorry I lied. I just didn't want to seem so pathetic in front of your friends."

"I was thinking—why don't you spend Thanksgiving at the Cape with me? We can fly there tomorrow, have some downtime, and get to know each other better. It will be fun."

The invitation caught me completely off guard.

"I . . ."

He cocked his head. "Was that 'yes'?"

"I didn't bring enough clothes for a long stay."

He glanced over at my suitcase. "Judging by the size of your bag, I thought you had packed for the rest of the year."

"Very funny. Women have to carry more things. And I don't have enough clothing."

"There are clothing stores in Cape Cod," he said. "Nice ones. And what better place to spend Thanksgiving than where it started? Plymouth is just thirty miles from my place."

"What about your brother? Will he be okay with me crashing your dinner?"

"He'll be thrilled to have a guest, since I'm as boring as stuffing."

"I like stuffing."

"There will be stuffing. Then you'll come?"

"I'd love to."

He looked genuinely excited.

"How's the oatmeal?" I asked.

"It's good. How's your Benedict?"

"It's better than IHOP."

"I would hope so." He drank his espresso shot, then set down the glass. "I might need a little more fuel. We have a busy day today."

"I thought you had the day off. We can't just stay here?"

"I have it off, I just thought you might like to see the city. Was there anything in particular you wanted to do?"

"Just be with you."

"That's a given."

I thought about it. "I'd like to see Radio City Music Hall and Central Park. Maybe go up the Empire State Building."

"Noted." He looked at his watch. "We should get ready. It's ten fifteen. Can you be ready to leave by eleven?"

"Yes, sir."

"I'll be back to claim you then."

We kissed and he went back to his room. I stole one of his leftover candied walnuts, then got in the shower.

CHAPTER

FIFTEEN

How can a robin egg blue box bring so much happiness?

Beth Stilton's Diary

It was a familiar pain in my stomach. About twelve years earlier, when the pain first manifested, it was diagnosed as irritable bowel syndrome by my doctor at the VA. This diagnosis was later changed to a stress disorder related to PTSD.

Lee arrived dressed casually in a navy-blue funnel-neck overcoat, over a light blue zippered sweater over an ivory-white tee. The blue made his eyes stand out. Maybe it was just me, but he looked movie-star handsome.

I was wearing my narrow-waisted black Canada Goose down jacket over a taupe-colored knit dress.

"You look nice," I said.

"You look very nice. Shall we go?"

The doorman called a cab forward and opened the door for me. Lee handed him a bill, then climbed in the other side. I still didn't know where we were going.

"Tiffany on Fifth, please," he said.

I turned to him. "Tiffany?"

"Just a little holiday shopping," he said.

The cab stopped across the street from the store. The sidewalk was crowded, especially in front of their holiday-themed window displays, which were cordoned off by brass stanchions connected by red-velvet ropes.

"They unveiled their window displays yesterday," Lee said. "Hence the crowds."

He led me to the front door, which was opened for us by a sturdy doorman.

"What are you looking for?" I asked.

"Something for you," he said.

"Me?" I had assumed he was getting something generous for Laurie or Carlie.

"Do you own anything from Tiffany?"

"No."

"In my opinion, at least once in every woman's lifetime, she should be gifted something in a Tiffany blue box. Do you own a pearl necklace?"

"You're not getting me a pearl necklace."

"I wasn't really asking permission; I was asking if you had one."

I crossed my arms. "No. I don't."

"Then that's where we begin. Every woman needs a pearl necklace. It goes with everything."

"Excuse me," he said to a gentleman standing near us. "Could you help me with some shopping?"

"I would be delighted to, sir. What can I help you with?"

"A pearl necklace to start."

"Excellent. My name is Earl."

Rhymes with *pearl*, I thought.

"I'm Lee, and this is my friend Beth."

"Lee and Beth. My pleasure." Earl led us to the corner of the main floor where there was a glass case with pearl jewelry, earrings, necklaces, bracelets, and rings. He walked behind the counter to open the case.

"If I may, the silver-and-pearl necklace with our inspired key ring and *Return to Tiffany* label has been very popular."

"I'm thinking something a bit more traditional. A little more Audrey."

Earl smiled at the reference. "Yes, Miss Hepburn certainly wore them elegantly. To this day she is still our greatest salesperson." He pointed to a necklace. "How about this one?"

It was a simple strand of pearls. "We call this Tiffany Essential Pearls. It is eighteen inches long with Akoya cultured pearls with an eighteen-karat white gold clasp."

"Could I see it?"

"Absolutely." He reached into the case and brought it out. Lee took it from the man's white cotton-gloved hands and looked at me. "Would you mind trying this on?"

I took off my coat.

"I'll take that, ma'am," the salesman said. I handed my coat to him, then took the necklace from Lee and put it on. I peered into the oval mirror on the counter. It was the most beautiful jewelry I had ever worn.

"Oh, that's lovely," Earl said.

"She's lovely," Lee said. "How much is that?"

"It's twenty-seven fifty, sir."

"It's almost three thousand dollars," I said.

"You're right," he said. "Do you have something a little nicer?"

"We have the Tiffany Essential with the seven, seven five millimeter pearls."

"How big are these?"

"They are around six millimeters."

"Let's try the bigger one."

He brought one over.

"That's better," Lee said. "How much is this?"

"It's thirty-five, sir." Lee clasped the pearls around my neck. "Do you like them too?"

"I love them," I said.

"I like them too. Is there anything else I should see?"

"Similar to this, we have the Tiffany South Sea Noble necklace."

"What's the difference with that one?"

"It's the pearl, sir. But they begin in the forty-thousand-dollar range."

"I won't wear it," I said. "If you buy that, I'll never wear it. I would be too afraid."

Lee looked at me with amusement. "All right, the lady has spoken. Find us some matching earrings, and that will be good for now."

"Would you like to come pick them out?" Earl asked.

"No, I trust you."

"Very good, sir. Thank you. And if I might ask, Mr. Lee, are you an author?"

Lee glanced around; it was the one time I noticed him reticent to share who he was. "Yes."

"Forgive me, I understand your desire for privacy, I just want to tell you that I have very much enjoyed reading your books. Thank you for the hours of entertainment."

"You're welcome," Lee said.

Earl left us, returning about ten minutes later with two Tiffany blue boxes, only one of them wrapped with ribbon. "Would the lady like to wear that beautiful necklace out of the store?"

I looked at Lee. "Can I?"

"Absolutely," he said. "We have lunch reservations upstairs; I think that would be appropriate."

Lee had made reservations at the Blue Box Café, Tiffany's upstairs restaurant. The room was, as expected, decorated all in robin egg blue with hundreds of Tiffany boxes dangling from the ceiling. The thought that I had even stepped foot in this world was dizzying; every time my hand strayed to touch the pearls around my neck, I felt my heart pounding.

"I'll have to take you to breakfast sometime," he said. "Then you could say you had breakfast at Tiffany's."

"Who would I tell?"

"Maxine," he said. We both laughed.

"Would your friend Frankie be impressed?"

"Absolutely. She's a Hepburn fan."

"Who isn't?"

I had the Coquille St. Jacques, a Maine sea scallop with cauliflower. Lee ordered the Croque aux Truffes, the grilled truffled ham and cheese sandwich. We shared a bowl of chilled corn soup with jumbo lump crab and jalapeño.

As we were finishing eating, Lee said, "You still haven't seen your earrings."

He reached into the Tiffany bag and brought out a box tied up with ribbon. I untied it, opened the box, then brought out a rectangular blue velvet box and opened it. The pearls shone against the velvet, along with the diamond marquis crosses on top of them.

"Oh," I said. "They're beautiful." I looked up. "Are those real diamonds?"

"Of course."

"How much were they?"

"You don't look a gift horse in the mouth."

"You do when it has diamond teeth."

He smiled at that. "It was a little more than the necklace."

"How little?"

"A little more than double."

I shut the box. "That's too much."

"Beth, the problem isn't that it's too much, the problem is you don't think you deserve to own something that much."

His words stopped me. I looked down at my necklace. "You're right. I'm sorry. I'm not good at accepting gifts. I haven't much practice."

"Thank you for letting me experience this with you." He got up, walked over to me, and put the earrings on. He kissed my forehead, then sat back down.

After he sat I asked, "What could I possibly give you?"

"Something money can't buy," he said. "That's what I want."

"And what would that be?"

"That's for you to decide."

I gazed into his eyes for the longest time, then said, "This will be fun."

He went back to eating. Then he looked up again. ". . . And for the record, spoiling you is fun for me too. It's better to give than to receive."

Only if you get to receive sometimes too, I thought.

CHAPTER

SIXTEEN

There are times when my brain is carjacked by the past, and all I can do is wait to see where my demons abandon the car.

Beth Stilton's Diary

We finished lunch, then headed off to our next engagement. He gave me the Tiffany bag to carry, since he said it would attract envy.

As we walked over to Sixth Avenue I asked, "Back to your publisher?"

"Close. You said you wanted to see Radio City Music Hall."

"Oh, that's right, they're next to each other."

"Yes. And if you noticed the color of the Empire State Building yesterday, it was red and green, celebrating the opening of the Radio City Rockettes Christmas Spectacular." He held up two tickets. "I got us tickets."

"Of course you did." We walked into the VIP entrance. "I just told you this morning! How do you get all these tickets?"

"Nothing is ever really sold out."

"Not when you're J. D. Harper."

"There might be some truth to that. And Laurie has connections." As we walked into the lobby, Lee said, "Do you know who performed here last night?"

"No idea."

"Your Barry Manilow. I'm surprised you didn't sleep out for the show."

"You're never going to let me live that down. I was thirteen."

"I wonder if they have any T-shirts left. I'm going to ask."

"I won't wear it." Then I grinned. "Maybe I will."

"You'll wear a Barry Manilow T-shirt, but you won't wear a forty-thousand-dollar pearl necklace."

"No one would steal the T-shirt."

❄ ❄ ❄

Fortunately, I guess, the Barry Manilow people had taken their merchandise with them, though an overly helpful usher told Lee where he could find some contraband Barry Manilow paraphernalia a few blocks over.

The theater was even more grandiose than I imagined. The hall was brilliantly lit with roving snowflakes projected on the ceiling. My heart was pounding and I think I was as excited as the children to be there. Lee must have felt the same way, because he said, "I haven't been here for years. I feel like a child again."

I smiled. "This is exciting. Thank you for bringing me."

We were seated near the stage, and only a few people stopped Lee on the way to our seats, though I noticed a dozen or more people sneaking pictures, some more clandestine than others. One man walked right up to the end of our row, pointed his camera at Lee and took his picture, then walked away. I thought it was rude, but Lee just took it in stride.

When the theater bell rang, signaling that the curtain was about to rise, Lee said to me, "If it's not too much, I thought that after the show we could take a carriage ride through Central Park. It's cold, but they have big blankets to cuddle in."

I smiled. "That sounds especially nice."

"After, we could go back to the hotel for dinner, then just watch a movie."

"What movie?" I asked.

He grinned and repeated my words from last night. "Does it matter?"

The first sounds of the orchestra reverberated through-out the bowl as the curtain rose, displaying a dazzling back-drop of lights and dancers.

The show lasted ninety minutes with singing, dancing, and a live Nativity. It was fun watching the children around me, especially when the camels from the Nativity came on-stage followed by the grand appearance of Santa Claus.

Near the end of the show, a row ahead of me and just a few seats over, a little girl was crying. I don't know why; she was probably tired or hungry or maybe just overstimulated, but her mother kept slapping her hand and telling her to shut up. I watched them. The anger and annoyance in her mother's eyes were too familiar to me.

Her mother glanced around to make sure no one was watching, then she surreptitiously reached over and vio-lently pinched the skin under the child's arm. The child's eyes went wide with pain. The mother slapped her hand over the little girl's mouth, yanked her from her seat, and carried her out of the theater.

I don't know if it was even real, but I could suddenly smell the vinegar odor of cheap whiskey on someone's breath. At that moment I was transformed out of the theater. I could hear my mother screaming at me. I was on the ground, on my stomach, my pants pulled down to my knees, my stepfather above me. I could smell the reek of his breath and the stinging pinch and grab of his perpetually oil-stained hands. He kept saying, "You're just trash like the rest of us."

When I came out of the flashback, I was trembling and sweating, and my stomach was growling and undulating. I felt like I was going to vomit.

"I need to go," I blurted out to Lee.

He looked at me with a concerned expression. "Are you okay?"

Without answering, I bustled my way out of our row and ran out of the theater to the restroom. I ran into a stall and threw up, barely making it to the bowl in time. My stomach continued to contract, and I threw up again, all that lovely food pouring into the toilet.

A kind voice behind me asked, "Are you okay?"

I managed a "Yes," but I wasn't. I was having a severe panic attack. When I felt like I was done vomiting, I locked the stall door, hung my coat on the door's hook, and sat on the toilet, pulling my knees up to my chest. I was panting heavily, and my forehead was wet with sweat.

About fifteen minutes later my phone rang. It was Lee.

"Are you okay?"

"I'm in the bathroom. I'm sick."

"I'm sorry. I'm out in the lobby. Take your time."

I knew when the show ended because the bathroom filled with women. People kept grabbing the handle on my stall and rattling it to see if it was really locked. I hid inside the stall like a public womb, shaking and isolated from the crowds. One woman even looked between the crack in the door to see if someone was in there. She quickly withdrew.

The crowd eventually dwindled. It was probably close to a half hour when I finally got off the toilet. I got my coat, then went out to a sink and washed my face and hands, then washed the vomit out of my hair. I drank from the sink to rinse out my mouth. I desperately wished I had a breath mint or some gum.

When I came out of the bathroom, the lobby was mostly deserted except for the janitorial staff cleaning up after the last crowd and Lee, who was leaning up against the wall talking to a security officer. He held my Tiffany bag in the crux of his arm.

When he saw me, he immediately shook the man's hand to excuse himself, then walked quickly to me. His face showed his concern.

"You look pale. Are you okay?"

I nodded. "My stomach hurts."

"Probably too much rich food," he said. "I'm sorry, I should have taken it easier on you."

"It's not that. I just don't feel well. My stomach hurt this morning." I looked at him. "I didn't want to ruin everything."

"You haven't ruined anything. Let's get you back to the hotel. I'll get you some tea. The hotel will have something for your stomach."

Lee hailed us a cab, and I lay quietly against him on the way back to the Mark. My stomach began hurting and gurgling again, but it was nothing compared to the pain and worthlessness that had crept inside my chest. Equal to the joy and light of the day was the despair I now felt. I wanted to vanish into nothing.

When we got back to the hotel, Lee followed me into my

room as I went into the bathroom and stood over the toilet again. After a few minutes I took off my clothes and changed into my nightshirt. Then I brushed my teeth and gargled the entire bottle of mouthwash the hotel had provided.

"What can I do for you?" Lee asked as I came out. He had already pulled the sheets down on my bed and arranged the pillows. "I ordered you some chamomile tea to calm your stomach. It will be right up."

"I think I just need to sleep," I said.

"Let me help you into bed."

I crawled into the bed, and he pulled the sheets up to my waist, then kneeled down next to me.

"Does your stomach still hurt?"

"Not as much."

"The tea will help." He took my hand.

"Is my breath okay?"

"It smells like you downed an entire bottle of mouthwash."

Despite my pain and sadness I smiled. "I did."

"I thought so." He put his hand on my forehead. "You're a little warm. Are you sure you're okay?"

I closed my eyes tightly, pinching water from them. He wiped the tears with his hands.

"Do you want me to spend the night with you?"

I felt so awful, but I shook my head. "I'm sorry."

"It's okay."

Just then the room's doorbell rang.

"There's your tea. Let me get that." He opened the door, signed the check, then came back with a tray with the cup and some sweeteners. "I'm going to put some honey in it. It's good for your stomach." He poured some honey into the cup and stirred it with a spoon. He tested it for heat.

"Okay, it's a little hot, so just sip it. It will help. Your stomach and your heart."

I sat up and took the cup with both hands and sipped it. It tasted sweet and good. I took another sip, then handed him back the cup. "Thank you."

He set the cup on the nightstand. "You're welcome. You're sure you don't want me to stay with you?"

"I'll be okay."

He smiled at me sadly, then said, "Okay then. You sleep well." He pulled the blankets up to my chin, leaned over me, and kissed my forehead. "Sickness aside, today was a good day. One of the best of my year. Thank you for spending it with me." He looked into my eyes. "You're going to get a lot of downtime in the Cape, okay? I promise I'll take good care of you. I'll pamper you."

"You're the one who should be pampered," I said.

"I get pampered enough." He pressed his index finger above the bridge of my nose and slowly rotated it. "Our flight isn't until noon tomorrow, so we have plenty of time. Just sleep in. Let me know when I can come over. If you need anything in the night, I'm right next door."

I smiled at him and he kissed me again.

"Thank you for being so good to me," I said. "I don't know why you are so good to me."

He looked at me quizzically. "I don't know why you wouldn't know why." He leaned over, kissed me one more time on the forehead. "Sleep well." He walked out the door.

CHAPTER

SEVENTEEN

Sometimes I feel like my memories should come with Graphic Content and NSFW warnings.

Beth Stilton's Diary

I'm not surprised that things turned as quickly as they did. On a dark, almost subconscious level, I'm sure I anticipated it. I don't know if it's superstition, PTSD, or a sadistic universe that hates me, but whenever something goes well in my life, I know there will be a reconciling. Something bad will happen. It always does. So it goes.

I hadn't always resigned myself to being so pessimistic. In fact, I spent many years fighting the gravity of my former hardships. But as hard as I tried to leave it behind, my adult life experiences only proved that I was inseparably linked to the experiences of my past. No matter how hard I tried, I could not make things better.

I joined the military to be strong and secure. I got raped. I got married to a man I thought I loved, and he turned into a monster I didn't recognize. I was blissful when I learned I was pregnant—to finally have someone to love who would love me back. Then I lost the baby. There's an obvious pattern at work.

I suppose it wouldn't take Freud to decipher the underlying belief of that pattern. Even a shallow dive into my childhood would reveal that I had never been enough. For anyone. And people who aren't enough are unworthy of good things happening to them. It's simple math, really. The relationship with Lee was a good thing that happened to me. Therefore, it was destined to fail.

I didn't sleep that night. I had too much on my mind. Mostly, I had Lee on my mind. I had never been treated so well by a man so good. He was beyond my comprehension.

I didn't stay awake just because of all that was on my mind, but also because I was afraid to sleep—well, to dream. I had been in this state many times before, and I knew what monsters lay waiting behind the screen of consciousness. My nightmares were so dark that I could barely stand to recall them myself—I'd certainly never shared them with another soul. Someone as kind and caring as Lee couldn't handle knowing what a mess I was; if he ever found out, he'd leave—and my heart would be the most broken thing about me.

That night, one particularly haunting memory found its way to the theater of my mind. I was still an EMT then, and my partner and I had arrived at the scene of an accident where the car had caught fire. The fire department had just put out the flames, and I was sent in to verify the bodies. The air was filled with the pungent stench of burned plastic and flesh.

There were two people in the front seat, mercifully dead, as they were both charred beyond recognition. As horrific as that was, I saw a baby seat in the back with the infant still strapped inside. I opened the car's back door and climbed across the wire frame of the melted seat to the infant. The baby was charred like the bodies in front. Then, to my horror, I saw the baby's chest rise.

"The baby's alive!" I shouted. "Get me morphine. Quick."

My partner handed me a syringe. I pushed the needle into the child's burnt leg. Within seconds, the breathing stopped. I felt the child's wrist. There was no longer a pulse. I turned back to my partner. "You gave me too much."

His gaze was heavy and dark. "I know."

I have dreamed of that moment more times than I can remember. I see myself in a room surrounded by charred faces. Sometimes they cry, sometimes they scream at me. And that's just one of the episodes airing on my nocturnal network. There are others, equally horrific.

That is me. The real me. This is what Lee didn't know about me and I never wanted him to find out. The universe had never been my friend, and now it was just mocking me with a mirage of happiness that could never last.

They say the higher you climb, the harder you fall, and right now, I was at a dizzying height. I knew that I could never survive a fall from this height. I had to get out while I could.

At four in the morning, I got dressed, packed up all my things, then, on the hotel's notepad, wrote Lee a final note.

> My dear Lee,
> How do I tell the most beautiful man I've ever met
> how sorry I am? Or how grateful I am for all the
> kindness and love you have shown me?
> You are truly a gift to this world. My gift to you is
> to free you from me.
> I know me. You deserve better.
> Love, Beth

I cried as I wrote the note, but I knew that when we inevitably ended, it was better to end on my terms. That's how I had survived. And my life was about nothing more than survival. Love was a luxury, and right now I was more in love than I had ever felt in my life. But to be in love is to be vulnerable, and that was something I could not afford.

I folded the note in two, then took my bag and walked out of my room, slowly closing the door so that he wouldn't hear it. The hallway was lit but quiet. I crouched down and quietly slid the note under Lee's door, then took the elevator downstairs.

A doorman greeted me as I came out of the elevator. "You're up early. May I help you with your bags?"

I wiped my eyes, hoping that he wouldn't notice that I had been crying, but I'm sure I was way beyond that. "I need to go to the train station. Is it far from here?"

"Too far to walk. Penn Station is about three miles. But I have a cab available right outside."

"Do you know if there's a train to Lancaster?"

"Let's ask the desk. They know everything. What's your name?"

"It's Beth Stilton."

A tired but elegant-looking Black woman was standing behind the counter. She smiled at me as we approached.

"Aria, Ms. Stilton needs to catch a train, but she doesn't know the train schedule."

I could tell when she noticed I was crying because her expression softened. "Let's see what we have." She typed something into her computer. "What is your destination, Ms. Stilton?"

"Lancaster, Pennsylvania."

"Pennsylvania," she said, still looking at her screen. "Here it is. The next train to Lancaster from Penn Station leaves at four forty-five. The train after that is seven thirty. But I think we need to get you on the first one, don't we?"

I nodded. "If we could."

"You have thirty-five minutes; you should be okay. It's forty-nine dollars. Would you like me to purchase the ticket for you?"

"Yes, please."

I handed her a credit card. She scanned it in. She suddenly looked perplexed. "Hm." She turned to me. "I'm sorry, there seems to be a problem with this card. Do you have another one you'd like to use?"

I felt embarrassed. "Yes," I said, digging into my wallet.

"You have a card on file. I could put the ticket on your room."

"I'd rather not do that."

"No problem," she said gently. I handed her another card. Thankfully, that one worked.

"Would you like the ticket on your phone, or would you like me to print it out?"

I didn't want to turn my phone on. "Print it out, please."

She handed me a paper with my ticket. "There you go, dear. Have a beautiful day."

I was about to turn away when I remembered the gifts. I reached into my suitcase and took out the Tiffany bag with the two beautiful blue boxes inside. "Would you see that Mr. Harper gets these, please?"

She lightly frowned as she took the bag from me. "Of course. I'll put them in the safe."

The ride to Lancaster was just shy of three hours. The passengers around me looked as tired as I was. I noticed someone reading Lee's book. She seemed completely engrossed. I turned away. I wondered if I would ever be able to read his books again. I doubted it. It would be too much like being with him.

I fell asleep somewhere before Philadelphia and fortunately woke just twenty minutes before arriving in Lancaster. I dragged my bag into the crowded station, got a Diet Coke from a machine, then just sat on a bench and held my phone, afraid to turn it on. I needed to call for an Uber, but I knew the moment I woke my phone that the texts and messages would start.

I took a deep breath, then turned it on. As I waited for the phone to reboot, it suddenly started dinging with texts and voicemail messages. I couldn't help but see the first messages. They were all from Lee, asking me to call him.

I ordered the Uber, then put my phone in my pocket and went out to wait for the car. The air was cold, probably in the low thirties, and a slight breeze braced my cheeks. It felt good.

The city was busy. Lancaster, with its Dutch and Amish influence, is a popular destination during the holiday season. It would only get busier as the season neared—as people would come from all over the country to celebrate Christmas here. And I would just ignore it.

After I got home, I heated myself a bowl of tomato soup

for lunch with a cheese sandwich, then I turned on my phone. Lee had called three times and texted four times. The last text he sent he had just learned from the desk that I had checked out and left his gifts. He begged me to just talk to him. But I couldn't.

CHAPTER

EIGHTEEN

Far too often we are so fearful of failure that we embrace it.

Beth Stilton's Diary

There was the usual uptick at work. Cyberattacks and crime always increase during the holidays. I was glad to keep busy dealing with other people's problems. It's easier to solve problems when you don't have your own skin in the game. The truth is, I was in excruciating pain. I thought my heart couldn't be more broken than it already was, but I was very wrong.

Frankie called. I hadn't talked to her for a while, and she was blown away by all she'd missed. She was completely impressed that J. D. Harper had wanted to date me. She took me out for a drink. I cried. A lot. I could do that with her. In the end she reassured me that I had probably done the right thing. *Probably*. She invited me to share Thanksgiving with her and her husband, Arlo. I accepted.

I also heard from two of the book club women, Maxine and Pauline, who reached out to see how I was doing—or how Lee and I were doing. Pauline was sad to hear we'd gone our separate ways. She said, "I just really thought that was going to work out like one of his books." To my surprise, she invited me to join her family for Thanksgiving. I told her that I had accepted another invitation, but I was so very grateful for hers. I really was. I'm sure it would have been as delightful as it was extravagant.

Maxine, on the other hand, was just short of outright giddy. "I guess we'll have to stop reading his books," she said.

"Why would you say that?" I asked.

"For him to use you like that, then leave you? What a repulsive man."

"He's not repulsive. And why would you assume he left me?" I asked.

"Because only a fool would leave him. And you're not a fool." She paused, then said, "Are you?" Then she asked, "You wouldn't still have his phone number, would you?"

Monday morning, I was still in my yoga pants and T-shirt when my doorbell rang. I figured it was the UPS man with my supplements. It wasn't. Lee was standing in my doorway.

"May I come in?" he asked.

I was still stunned by his presence and didn't answer.

"Please. It's a little cold."

"I'm sorry. Come in." I stepped back from the door.

He walked in, took something from his pocket, and put it on the dining room table. It was the note I left him in the hotel.

"Since you're not answering my calls, the last communication I had from you was this note, so I thought we should probably start with that. We'll go one line at a time." He lifted the note. "'My dear Lee.'" He looked at me. "That part's okay."

He continued reading. "'How do I tell the most beautiful man I've ever met how sorry I am?'" He looked at me. "To his face. You tell him to his face and let him respond. You let him plead or beg or whatever, but you give him that chance."

"So, I'm a coward," I said.

"That you're not. I think it's more that you're a pleaser. And you didn't want to see me hurt. Am I right?"

I nodded.

"I can forgive that. Next line. 'Or how grateful I am for all the kindness and love you have shown me.'"

He looked up. "The answer to that isn't difficult either. You show your gratitude for kindness and love by giving it back. It's really that simple. And up until you left this note, you were doing a good job of that. I felt very loved and very appreciated."

"Next line. 'You are truly a gift to this world. My gift to you is to free you from me.' Okay, first part, again, very simple. This isn't about the world, it's about two people. It's about a boy and a girl who are in love. It's about us. The world be damned.

"Second part, 'My gift to you is to free you from me.'" He looked up. "This line is very confusing. If I understand this correctly, your gift to me is to take yourself away from me? That literally makes no sense. But putting that aside, since you gave me back the gifts I gave you, I likewise give you back your gift, and unfree myself from you. So, here I am."

I thought that was pretty brilliant.

"Next line. 'I know me. You deserve better.'" He shook his head. "Two points here. First, I don't think you know yourself at all. I think you know a lot of what some other people told you about yourself, and you foolishly believed them. Because the Beth I know is warm, beautiful, and generous and, with the exception of my broken heart, wouldn't hurt a soul.

"Second part, no one, except for me, can decide what I deserve. Not you. Not anyone."

"All right. Last line. 'Love, Beth.' This line is okay too. But only if it's true." He looked me in the eyes. "Is it true? Do you love me?"

My eyes welled up with tears. I nodded.

"Then why did you leave me?"

I was quiet for a long time, then I said, "The woman you saw last Friday wasn't sick. She's broken. I had a flashback at the Rockettes. I felt myself being abused by my stepfather. Then my body shut down. I was in a full-scale panic attack." I looked into his eyes. "I know I act strong, but I'm not. And I knew that once you discovered who I really am, you wouldn't like me anymore. I wouldn't be able to take that."

"You thought it might break, so you broke it first."

I nodded.

"But it wasn't breaking."

"It will. It always does. But especially with us."

"Why especially with us?"

"It's obvious. You're J. D. Harper. I'm nothing. I'm garbage."

His eyes flashed. "Don't ever say that again."

"If you knew how deep my brokenness really is, you would turn and run."

For what seemed a long time he just stared at me, his expression wavering between sadness and anger. Then he said, "I want to show you something." He took off his shirt. Then, holding his shirt in his hands he said, "Do you remember when we first met, you asked if I had any tattoos? I told you mine were more of a . . . brand." He slowly turned around.

I gasped. His entire back was deeply scarred. He looked as if he'd fallen in a fire.

"What happened?"

He turned back around. "The mother who did this to me said I should tell anyone who asked that I fell asleep on a radiator." He put his shirt back on. "You're not the only one who's had a hard life, Beth, or is deeply broken.

"You said there are younger and prettier women out there, but do you think I would fit with someone who has never known real pain? That I could be intimate with someone whose idea of suffering is slow internet or a broken fingernail?

"It's that very brokenness you're afraid of showing me that drew me to you. And sometimes, when two broken people come together, those jagged pieces just fit. That's what *Bethel* was about. That's why it spoke to you. It was about two people finding light in the darkest of moments. It's about hope.

"I don't know the future. Maybe we're a match, maybe we're not. Maybe it will be you who decides I've got too much baggage to live with. Or just too many scars. Because some of the worst scars I carry, you can't see.

"But after I left you that first time, I felt something different, a feeling I didn't recognize. Then I realized what it was. I felt homesick. I was literally pining for you.

"Carlie said it was nothing, that you were just another beautiful fan, and I've been on the road too long. She said I'd get over it by the next tour city."

"I knew I didn't trust her," I said.

"Well, she was wrong, because it just got worse. Your face was graffitied all over my brain like a New York subway."

I suddenly laughed. He smiled. "It was that bad. I'm on national television, and all I could think about was you."

"You were really thinking of me?"

"I really was."

I put my head down so he wouldn't see my eyes welling with tears.

"Beth, I didn't come just to talk to you. I came to bring you back with me. I'd love to make this your moment when the sun finally shines. But only you can decide if you're going to open your arms and embrace it or run from it because it might not last. No one can make that decision but you.

"Just consider that maybe this is also *my* moment of sunlight. That *I'm* the lucky one. Because that's what it feels like to me. Since I met you, it's like the clouds parted.

"Please, Beth. Trust me. Give me a chance. Give *us* a chance. We've both suffered enough. Come back to the Cape with me." He gently put his hand on my chin and lifted my face until he looked directly into my eyes. "Say yes."

I met his gaze, then brought my mouth to his. When we broke the kiss at last, all I said was, "Yes."

CHAPTER

NINETEEN

*Napoleon said, "In victory, you deserve champagne;
in defeat, you need it," which is essentially the same
thing that Lee said to me on the flight to the cape.*
Beth Stilton's Diary

Lee helped me pack up my things and shut down the house. I left one light on in the kitchen and set the thermostat just high enough that my pipes didn't freeze while I was away. I honestly didn't know how long I'd be gone—I assumed less than a week, until he went back out on the road, but, as he had in New York, Lee told me to keep my options open.

We took the car service to the Lancaster airport, where Lee had chartered a plane to take us to his home in Cape Cod. I had never been on a private jet before. I admit it was kind of thrilling, especially skipping the whole TSA pat-down thing.

After we were airborne, Lee brought out a gilded champagne box along with two crystal champagne flutes. He opened the box and took out a bottle.

"I brought this to celebrate you coming back with me. Louis Roederer, Cristal 2008. It was an exceptional vintage." He handed me the bottle to examine.

"Just the box looks expensive."

"Some wine experts gave it a perfect score. They call it a masterpiece."

"We're drinking a Van Gogh."

"Not quite. But it is very good. I was saving it for a special occasion." He smiled at me. "You coming home with me is a very special occasion."

"What if I had said no?"

"I would have drunk the whole bottle myself to commiserate, and they would have had to carry me off the plane. Either way it serves a purpose." He poured me a glass before pouring his own. "To us," he said, lifting the glass.

"To the broken," I said.

He smiled. "To the broken." We clinked glasses.

I took a sip. It was delicious. "This is lovely." I took another small sip, then said, "So, I'm going to meet your brother."

"Speaking of broken people," he said.

"He's broken too?"

"We're all broken."

"What's his name?"

"Marcus. He goes by Marc."

"What's he like?"

A short, amused grin crossed his face. "You'll find out. He's definitely his own person. He's very smart and very funny. Comedian funny. He's also a Civil War buff. He collects Civil War artifacts."

"Like the figurines you told me about when we first met."

"I help him collect those. It's his hobby, not mine, but it's something I can help him with. Other than that, we're a lot alike. We look alike. If he goes to town, people always ask for autographs or pictures with him."

"Does he go along with it?"

"No. He's mortified by it. That's one of the reasons he rarely leaves the house. He's very private."

"So he'll be around the house the whole time I'm there."

"You can count on it."

"Good, I'll get to know him."

"Maybe. You probably won't see much of him."

"Even in the same house?"

"It's a big house. And he'll keep to his own space. Especially with you there."

I set down my drink. "I thought you said he was glad I was coming."

"He is. But like I said, he's very private. Nothing personal, that's just him." He took a drink of champagne, then said, "Trust me. If he didn't like you, you wouldn't see him at all."

"Have the two of you always lived together?"

"For much of our lives, but not always. When I finally left for college, he signed up for the army to get out of the house."

"Good, he's an army vet. We'll have that in common."

"He won't want to talk about it. He didn't have a particularly good experience."

"Then we'll have that in common too."

"He only served two years, then got out. When he came back, he moved in with me until he got married."

"He was married?"

"For a few years."

"It didn't work out?"

"It worked out well. It was the happiest I'd ever seen him. Until she passed away. That's when he moved back in with me. We've been together ever since."

"How did she die?"

"A blood clot. It was sudden and unexpected."

"That's really sad." I studied his countenance. "You really care for him."

"More than I can say," he said. "I think of our relationship like soldiers in combat. Marc and I fought the same war. We had the same enemy."

"He's lucky to have you."

"We're lucky to have each other. I'm glad the two of you are finally going to meet."

CHAPTER

TWENTY

Lee's home is as large and luxurious as a private resort. Still, he seems a little uncomfortable in it, like someone wearing a tuxedo to a hockey match.

Beth Stilton's Diary

We landed around four o'clock at the Cape Cod Gateway airport. Lee had left his car there, and he carried my bag out to the nearby parking lot. I had expected he'd be driving a Bentley or Land Rover, but instead we approached a fully restored, vintage Ford Mustang convertible. It was baby blue with a white vinyl top and two-tone blue vinyl interior.

"This is what you drive?"

"It's a '66 Ford Mustang. It was a vintage year for the car."

"How long have you had it?"

"Technically, since it was made. My father left it to us when he died. It sat in the garage for thirty years. One of the first things I did when I sold that first book was to have it fully restored. I found a body shop at a Ford dealership in Detroit where they restored it to showroom specifications. The color is the original Acadian blue, and this was the first year the iconic Mustang was in the corral." He unlocked the trunk, then said, "I'm sorry, I'm boring you. I just geek out over old cars."

"The protagonist in your book *My Brother's Keeper* drove a blue convertible Mustang."

"Same car."

"I feel like I'm walking through a novel."

Unfortunately, it was too cold to drive with the top down.

Lee didn't live very far from the airport; a little over three miles. His home looked to me like a resort. It was on nine acres with more than a thousand feet of private sandy beach. The main house was large, more than ten thousand square feet, with a steeply pitched roof with a shingled turret and a watchtower. The garage was on the east side of the estate and separate from the house. It looked like a home itself with six separate bays.

It was stunningly beautiful.

"This is where you live?"

"Not enough, lately," he said. "Over there is Hyannis Harbor, some of the Kennedys' property. We're north of Martha's Vineyard and Nantucket Island."

The driveway circled to the front of the house, beneath an arched portico worthy of a hotel entrance. The outside of the home was white clapboard siding, except near the double front door entry that was done in stone.

Lee parked the Mustang in front of the house, and we got out.

"So this is how the other half lives."

"Not exactly half," he said.

He got my bag out of the trunk, and we walked inside. There was a sense of openness since the entryway ceiling rose nearly twenty feet to a round turret circled by windows and sporting a brass chandelier. There was an old-world, nautical feel to the place.

The floors and banisters were light oak, and the interior of the house, that which wasn't window, was white paneled wood with hints of aquamarine inside the panels.

"This is stunning."

"It's opulent," he said. "It's way too much."

"It cost too much?"

"Everything is too much. I could be happy in a log cabin. Laurie talked me into buying it. She said it was a 'steal' and a good investment. And Marc likes the seclusion. He said it feels like we're on an island." He set my bag down. "You can't beat the sunsets, though."

He picked a note up from the counter. "Looks like Marc made us dinner."

"I thought you said he doesn't cook."

"He doesn't. At least not often. I'll read what he wrote. 'Lasagna in the oven, peach balsamic salad in the fridge. Dinner for two. If you are alone, come get me.'" Lee nodded. "That was nice of him."

"Then he knows you went to get me."

"He knows all about you."

"You don't even know all about me."

"I know enough. The rest is window dressing."

"What?"

He laughed. "I'll show you to your room."

CHAPTER

TWENTY-ONE

You can tell a lot about an author by what he writes.
And what he doesn't.

Beth Stilton's Diary

y room was bright, on the south side of the house, the windows facing toward the bay. There was a king-sized bed with a white duvet cover and pale blue pillows. The headboard was taller than me, simple with a textured gray fabric cover. At the foot of the bed was a wicker chest.

"You've got your own bathroom and walk-in closet. Just make yourself at home."

"How many rooms are there in the house?"

"There are eight bedrooms and eleven bathrooms."

"You have eleven bathrooms?"

"I know. Go figure. I think whoever built this leviathan might have had a problem with incontinence.

"I'll show you around after dinner. If you want to put your things away, I'll get dinner out of the oven."

"Thank you. I won't be long."

After he left, I sat on the bed. I felt different than I had in New York. It wasn't just the privacy or setting. It was that I no longer felt the need to hide myself from him.

What I said to him about not knowing me was true. But the opposite was just as true. Other than the abuse he had shared, I knew little of the hardships he had faced as a child. The truth was, I knew more about him through his books than I did in real life. I was curious to see just how much the writer and the man aligned.

CHAPTER

TWENTY-TWO

I've already shared enough about myself for him to write a book. I'm anxiously waiting for the chance to thumb through his pages.

Beth Stilton's Diary

arc's lasagna was good, if not particularly authentic—he used cheddar cheese—but I'm hardly a connoisseur. I still considered store-bought frozen pizza a treat. What I loved most about dinner is that his brother had cooked for us, which just added to my eagerness to meet him.

After dinner Lee gave me a tour of the main floor. I loved the indoor pool and was looking forward to using it.

"I can swim in the morning?"

"You can swim whenever you want. There's a robe and pool slippers in your closet."

"This is more luxurious than the Mark."

"It's more private, at least."

The kitchen looked like something out of a magazine. Like the rest of the house, the room was white, except for the stove, which was stainless steel with a cobalt-blue front that matched the stove hood. The counters and backsplash were slabs of bluish-gray marble, and the fixtures were nickel-plated.

"I might even cook in a kitchen like this."

"There's the fridge and pantry. Help yourself to whatever you like. I'm going grocery shopping tomorrow, so if there's anything you need, just let me know."

We walked out of the kitchen back out into the dining room. "That's the nickel tour," he said.

"Are you going to show me the upstairs?"

"No. That's Marc's inner sanctum. Like I said, he likes his privacy."

"Noted. I'll stay on ground level." I sighed with pleasure. "I just can't believe how beautiful it is here. It's like we're alone on a desert island."

"That's a pleasant fiction," he said.

"Speaking of fiction, how's your book doing? Don't we find out tomorrow about the list?"

"There you go, breaking the spell."

"Sorry."

"It's doing well. My publicist called me last night. The media requests are stacking up, and my publisher is trying to get me to extend my tour into Canada."

Just hearing that made my stomach hurt. Not with anxiety, but sadness. I didn't want to be away from him. Still, I tried to sound happy for him.

"Canada's nice."

"Canada is nice. But not when I could be here with you."

I loved that he said that.

He took my hand. "Let's go watch the sunset."

We walked out one of the back doors about fifty yards across the grass to where two navy-blue Adirondack chairs were facing the ocean.

"Marc bought these chairs. They're called Adirondack, after the mountains in New York. *Adirondack* is a Mohawk word that literally means 'they who eat trees.'"

"How do you know these things? You would totally crush it on *Jeopardy!*"

He grinned. "I do a lot of research. It's my job to look for interesting things."

"Is there anything you don't know?"

"I don't know where you were born. And I'm still a little hazy about what you do for work."

"Work," I said. "Talk about breaking the spell. You know I'm AWOL. I didn't check in online at work today. It's your fault."

"Would you like me to write you a note?"

"I'll be okay. I'm that one employee without a life who always covers for everyone else, so they owe me."

"Tell me more about what you do," he said.

"I work in fraud analysis. I keep people from getting ripped off by cybercrooks."

"That's surprising."

"What did you think I did?"

"I thought you might be a massage therapist. Or a cyber-crook."

"Thanks."

"How did you get into that line of work?"

"I was good at math."

"That doesn't surprise me. People who come from abusive backgrounds gravitate toward things they can predict and control, ergo, mathematics."

"I was just trying to make money. After I divorced my husband, I went to school to become a bookkeeper. One of my instructors told me that I could make more in the field of fraud analysis. I ended up getting a bachelor's degree in forensic accounting."

"Beth Stilton, Cyber Detective. Taking the bad guys offline."

I laughed. "At least I've got job security. That's one thing about fraud, you know it's never going away."

"What kind of things does a cyber sleuth look for?"

"There's a whole gamut. Friendly fraud, clickjacking, write-off schemes, triangulation, return fraud, proxy piercing."

"I have no idea what any of that is. But I guess you're good with a computer."

"I spend more time with a screen than I do with humans."

"I think everyone does these days." He looked out into the horizon. "Tell me about your childhood."

"That was an interesting segue. I told you at coffee."

"You gave me the flap copy version."

"Where do you want me to begin?"

"Begin at the beginning and go on till you come to the end. Then stop."

"Okay, Lewis Carroll. I was born in Sellersville, Pennsylvania, which means nothing since my mother was basically a nomad and we were only there a few months. My mother just moved from town to town. After she got pregnant with me, she tried to settle down, but that didn't work out. So she moved again. With one exception, I don't remember ever living in the same place more than a couple months."

"Why was she so nomadic?"

"I think she was either chasing men or running from them. I'm sure alcohol played a part. She was a heavy drinker even before she dropped out of high school."

"What were her parents like?"

"Surprisingly normal and kind. During one stretch, I

stayed with them for almost a year. Those were the happiest days of my childhood."

"Those were your salad days," Lee said. "The halcyon years."

"Are you writing my story?"

"Maybe. Go on."

"My grandmother used to say to me, 'I'm sorry about your mother. We raised her the best we knew. We don't know what happened to her.'" I exhaled slowly. "I think that sometimes the wiring is just off in people's head."

"I would agree with that," Lee said.

"Nomad aside, she was mean as a snapping turtle, and her drinking just exacerbated that. I don't remember a time in my life when she didn't beat me. But the neglect was even worse. I was only six when I became the adult at home. I'd make her dinner, then clean up after. Most of the time she was passed out on the couch. When she wasn't, she was hungover or mean.

"Then she married Stan. It didn't seem possible, but things got worse. He was a drinker too. But he had other vices. He sexually abused me at least once a week from the time I was seven until I was fourteen. When I told my mother what he was doing, she hit me. Then Stan did too.

"He told me that if I ever told anyone again, he would skin me alive. To make his point, he brought home a rabbit he shot, and he made me hold it while he cut its skin off in front of me. He said that was exactly what he was going to do to me if I ever told anyone about us."

I could see anger grow in Lee's eyes.

"When I was twelve, I realized that the name Stan was just one letter away from Satan. I told myself that they must be related.

"A few years later, when I started middle school, I had to shower with the other girls at gym. One of the gym teachers noticed the bruising around my thighs and went to the school counselor. They brought me in and interrogated me until I finally told them what Stan was doing. They called the police and he was arrested.

"I had to testify against him in court. It was the most terrifying experience of my life. He started making these gestures in court like he was sharpening a knife.

"Unfortunately for Stan, the judge, the DA, and most of the jury saw him do it and the DA explained his threat about the rabbit. At that point I think the jury would have lynched him if they could. He spent seven years in prison."

"Have you seen him since?"

"Once. I saw him about a year after I got out of the military. We were coming out of a Walmart and I was with my new husband. We were in the parking lot and I pointed him out. My husband went after him. He took him to the side of the building, beat him up, and threw him in a dumpster."

"At least your husband was protecting you."

"I thought so at the time. The truth was, he was a bully and he relished the chance to beat up someone and come out a hero."

"Where's your mother today? Is she still alive?"

"I don't know. I cut off communicating with her years ago."

"And your biological father?"

"Same as my mother. He means nothing to me. I don't know if he's alive and I don't care." I looked at him. "Have you heard enough?"

"That's enough history for tonight."

The sun was setting to the west, and we both just silently looked out at the water.

"Some of the most beautiful sunrises and sunsets in the world are right here," he said.

"I read that the best place on the Cape to watch the sunrise is Lighthouse Beach in Chatham. What do you think?"

"I think the best place to watch a sunrise is with someone you love."

I turned and looked at him. "You're such a romantic."

"That's what they pay me for."

"I can't afford you."

He smiled. "We'll work something out."

CHAPTER

TWENTY-THREE

I met Lee's brother. The two of them look alike, but the interior wiring is scrambled differently. Maybe that comes from living in the shadow of a famous sibling.

Beth Stilton's Diary

The next morning, I woke earlier than usual. Even though I was in the same time zone as Lancaster, the sun rose nearly a half hour earlier and I was surprised to see that it was only 6:15. I got up and put my swimming suit on, then put on the robe and slippers and walked across the house to the pool area.

There were no lights on in the house, so I assumed everyone was still asleep. I waded into the pool. The water was warm enough to be comfortable but cool enough to refresh. I swam a few laps, then climbed into the hot tub to relax.

As I sat there in the bubbling hot water, I saw Lee walking down the beach. I got out of the tub, put on my robe, then went outside. The air was chilly, probably in the high forties, but I didn't care. I ran to him, my bare feet slipping in the dry sand.

"Lee!"

He turned and looked at me but said nothing. I realized that the man I was running to wasn't Lee.

When I was closer, I said, "I'm sorry, I thought you were someone else."

"You mistook me for Al," he said. "You must be Beth."

Al? "You must be Marc."

"Yes, it's nice to finally meet you."

"Lee said the two of you looked alike."

"People confuse us all the time. In town they ask me for his autograph."

"Sorry. From the pool, I thought you were him."

"No worries. I'm glad you'll be spending Thanksgiving with us. It's always nice to have company."

"Thank you. I'll let you get back to your walk." I was about to leave when I said, "Did you call him Al?"

"Of course. That's his name. Have a good day." He turned and continued his walk. I watched him for a little bit, then ran back to the house to get warm.

✳ ✳ ✳

I showered and dressed, then walked back out to the main room. Lee was in the kitchen chopping peppers.

"Good morning," I said as I leaned in to kiss him. "I met your brother."

"He came downstairs?"

"He was walking on the beach. I thought it was you."

He smiled. "I told you we look alike."

"You didn't tell me you were practically twins. Why does he call you Al?"

"Because it's my name."

"You have yet another name?"

He stopped chopping and turned to me. "Like you, I also go by my middle name. My first name is Albert. Albert Lee Heller. My mother thought by naming me after Albert Einstein, I might turn out smart."

"It worked."

"I never liked the name, so I started telling everyone my name was Lee."

"If Marc knows you hate the name, why doesn't he call you Lee?"

"Because he's called me Al since he could speak. And because Lee is also his name. My mother used her maiden name for our middle names. He's Marcus Lee Heller."

"This is getting confusing."

"Having three names is advantageous, really. If someone calls me J.D., I know it's a fan or a reporter. If they call me Albert, they're from the IRS or a spammer with a mailing list. And if they call me Lee, I know we're friends. It's like a secret code."

"How did you come up with J. D. Harper?"

"That's more interesting. Before I became an author, I worked for a PR firm. Sometimes people would hire us to come up with a name for a product. Coming up with a pen name is the same thing. You're trying to evoke a sense of familiarity. Take car names. Acura sounds like precision, Lexus is somewhere between luxury and sexual, Intrepid sounds courageous.

"It's the same thing with medicines. Aleve sounds like a combination of alleviate and relieve, which is what you're trying to do with pain.

"When I was trying to come up with a pseudonym, I wanted something with the same kind of flow as J. K. Rowling, who was the bestselling author in the world at the time. I took Harper from Harper Lee, and the initials J.D. have an intellectual quality, like the J.D. of Juris Doctorate. It also borrows on credibility from other great authors like J. D. Salinger and Nora Roberts's pseudonym, J. D. Robb."

"I never realized so much thought went into it."

"It doesn't always. Theodore Geisel came up with the pen name Seuss after he was banned from writing because he was caught drinking with a group of college students."

"Why would he be banned? College students are always drinking."

"It was during Prohibition. So he used his middle name, Seuss. It wasn't until many years later that he added the Dr." His expression lightened. "Did you know we say his name wrong? We say it like it rhymes with *moose*, when it should rhyme with *voice*. Soice."

"Dr. Soice. That sounds awful."

"That's the way he pronounced it. You, by the way, have a very good name for an author."

"Stilton? It's cheese."

"It's strong and memorable. So, other than my myriad names, did the two of you talk about anything interesting?"

"Not really. He did say that he was glad that I was spending Thanksgiving with you, because you don't get enough company."

"We don't. Laurie used to come with her partner, but now that both of their parents are older, that's on hiatus. I wish Marc would invite someone, but I don't know how he would even meet anyone, he's become such a recluse."

"I'd set him up with someone," I said. "If I knew anyone."

"You don't have any single friends?"

"I don't have any friends other than Frankie."

"What's she like?"

"She's addicted to tattoos, clove cigarettes, and rides a motorcycle. About four years ago, she met her man. Arlo. He's a hippie holdover from La Jolla."

"Arlo is the perfect name for a hippie. Or a folk singer. What does he do?"

"He's an artist. He makes jewelry from sea glass. Lately he's started dabbling in driftwood art."

"Driftwood and sea glass. Do you even have ocean?"

"We have Lake Erie."

"Regardless, she's married, so Frankie is out." He thought for a moment, then said, "Is Maxine single?"

Lee made breakfast for us—omelets with peppers, sweet jalapeños, and two kinds of cheese, white cheddar and Dubliner. It was delicious.

As we did the dishes, I asked, "What's our day like? It's Thanksgiving tomorrow. Do we have a lot of cooking to do, or are we eating out?"

"We cater," he said. "There's a resort nearby with a Thanksgiving take-out service called Turkeys to Go." He showed me the menu. "What do you think?"

"Last Thanksgiving, I had a frozen turkey potpie and a stale pumpkin chocolate chip cookie my friend Frankie made a week earlier. I won't be hard to please."

Later that afternoon, Lee had a television satellite interview, then we drove to the grocery store, which, no surprise, was crowded with Thanksgiving shoppers. We picked up the usual grocery items along with a frozen pizza for dinner. Also not surprisingly, the store had Lee's book for sale and our brief shopping excursion turned into a book event, as people asked for pictures and autographs. I wondered how he had done this for all these years.

I decided to make my own pumpkin chocolate chip cookies, so while Lee accommodated his fans, I called Frankie for the recipe, then bought those ingredients as well.

Laurie texted Lee around six.

> *Winter in Arcadia* still number one NYT.
> Sales climbing. Two movie offers.
> Jonathan doing monkey dance.

I had no idea what a monkey dance is, but it sounded exciting.

That night, Lee and I watched an old Bill Murray movie and ended up falling asleep together on the couch. My dreams were only sweet.

CHAPTER

TWENTY–FOUR

This was the most peculiar Thanksgiving of my life.
Also, the most enjoyable.

Beth Stilton's Diary

The next morning, I was making the cookies when Marc walked into the kitchen. He startled me, as Lee had gone to the UPS Store, and I forgot that I wasn't alone in the house. It was the first I'd seen him since I'd met him on the beach.

"Good morning, Beth."

"Good morning and happy Thanksgiving," I said.

"Happy Thanksgiving back. What are you making?"

"Pumpkin chocolate chip cookies."

"You're a sugar addict, aren't you?"

"Absolutely."

"Me too."

"Good. Now we can be friends."

A smile crossed Marc's face. "Where's Al?"

"He took a package to the UPS Store."

"Oh." He just looked at me for a moment, then said, "You're very pretty. I can see why he's attracted to you."

"Thank you. Are you always that direct?"

"I'm not verbose."

"Good, then can I tell you something?"

"You can tell me anything."

"I know how close the two of you are. I was just worried about you thinking—"

Before I could finish, he said, "That you're going to Yoko Ono us and break up the band?"

"Well, not quite what I was going to say."

"There's no problem. Al should have a girlfriend. He's been happier than usual."

Just then Lee walked in. We both stopped talking and looked at him. His eyes darted back and forth between us. "That's suspicious," he said. "Did I interrupt something?"

"No," I said. "We were just talking."

"We were talking about you," Marc said. "I was telling Beth how happy you've been acting since you met her. She was afraid I thought she was going to Yoko Ono us."

"I didn't say that," I said.

"Oh." Lee still seemed a little put off. "Well, don't go too heavy on that. I want to keep her on her toes."

I threw a chocolate chip at him.

A little before one, a delivery van pulled up with our meal. Lee went through the box to make sure we had everything, then we set everything out, transferring the food from tinfoil and cardboard containers to porcelain bowls and silver platters.

The three of us sat down. Lee poured wine into our glasses, then said, "Marc and I have a Thanksgiving tradition. Before we eat, we say something we're most thankful for. It can be more than one thing. Especially since we drink a toast each time."

"That's really sweet," I said.

"And then we say what we're most *not* thankful for. Which is also followed by a toast."

"Doesn't that defeat the purpose?" I asked.

"Don't mess with tradition," Marc said.

"Sorry," I said. "Who am I to mess with tradition?"

"Precisely," Marc said.

"I'll go first," Lee said. His expression turned more serious. "I'm grateful to be here with my two favorite people in the world. I didn't see this coming, but I usually don't. Life is like a car swerving around the semi into the oncoming lane of traffic. . . ."

"Whoa," I said. "That went south fast. . . ."

"My point exactly," Lee said. "Way too fast. Life *is* the unexpected."

"Are we still on the grateful thing?" I looked over at Marc. "Are we?"

Marc just shook his head, like I was in violation of a house rule.

"Sorry," I whispered.

Lee cleared his throat. "As I was saying, life is like that car coming around the semi into your lane of traffic. You never see what's going to hit you." He turned to me. "Beth, you're that car." He raised his glass. "To Beth."

"Thank you," I said. "I think."

Marc raised his glass. "To Beth. And other bad drivers."

"I'm not a bad driver," I said.

"That remains to be seen," Lee said.

I drank along with them, still not sure what to make of their tradition.

"What are you *not* grateful for?" Marc asked Lee.

He took a deep breath. "People who don't signal before they turn."

"Brilliant," Marc said. "I like how you kept with the bad drivers theme."

"Thank you. I was going for that."

Marc looked at me and raised his glass. "To bad drivers again."

"All right," I said. "I see how this is. I'll go next. What I'm grateful for . . ."

"It's not your turn," Marc said. "We go by age. I saw this meme the other day. A reporter was asking people what was the worst birthday present they ever received. Most of them were like, 'a diet plan' or 'a mouse pad.' But one of the respondents said, 'My life.'"

"That is so, so deep," Lee said.

"Like a really deep well," Marc said. "It's existential."

"Definitely existential."

"I'm lost," I said. "Is that what you're grateful for or not grateful for?"

Marc looked at me. "Neither. It was just something I saw online."

Lee chuckled.

"I'm getting serious now," Marc said. "I'm going to start with what I'm not grateful for. What I'm not grateful for is bees."

I looked back and forth between them. "Bees?"

"Each year bees kill more humans than spiders, centipedes, scorpions, venomous marine animals . . . and I don't need to remind you that we are on the water . . . and snakes, including pythons, cobras, and rattlesnakes, combined. In fact, bees are fifty-three times more deadly than sharks. And if that's not frightening enough, one stung me last week."

Lee laughed.

"Counterpoint," I said.

"This isn't *Face the Nation*," Marc said. "No debating."

"But we need bees. They pollinate. Without them we'd have no food. Like this meal in front of us wouldn't be here. This food that I'm hoping we might actually eat at some point."

"Oh," Marc said. "That's a very good point. Then bees are what I'm most grateful for."

Lee practically choked. When he could speak, he lifted his glass and said, "Two cheers."

We clinked and drank twice, then Lee said, "Now it's your turn, Beth."

"Wait," Marc said, lifting his hand. "I'm not finished. I have one more gratitude thing."

Marc cleared his throat. "I'm grateful for you being here, Beth. Because you make my brother happy. And that makes me happy."

I was surprised at how sweet he suddenly was. "Thank you. That was . . . lovely."

"And this is where the television audience goes, 'Ahhh,'" Marc said.

"You are really weird," I said to him.

"Yes, and now it's your turn. Try to keep up."

"Okay. I'm grateful to be here, in this beautiful house with two beautiful men, hopefully to share what looks to be a delicious meal that's getting colder by the minute."

"You're saying I'm beautiful," Marc said.

"Yes, that was implied."

"To beautiful me," Marc said, lifting his glass.

"To beautiful Marc," Lee repeated. We clinked glasses. Marc drained his.

"I need more wine," he said.

Lee poured more wine, then said to me, "Now tell us what you're not grateful for?"

"Things I'm not grateful for. People who do not clean up after their dogs."

"Amen," Marc said.

"And people who tell you about their hernia operation or pretty much any medical procedure you did not want to hear about."

"Preach it," Marc said.

"And one more thing. Eggplant. People act like it's edible. It's not."

Marc turned to Lee. "She's good."

Lee said, "I told you she was."

"She's totally going to fit in around here." He turned to me. "You're totally going to fit in, Yoko. Now stop talking and let's eat. The food's getting cold."

I just shook my head. It was by far the oddest and best Thanksgiving meal of my life.

CHAPTER

TWENTY–FIVE

I learned more about love in one moonlight walk than a thousand romance novels. It is a true irony, that the victory of love is found in surrendering to it.
Beth Stilton's Diary

That night, Lee and I took a moonlit walk along the beach. We held hands. It was cold, and he put my hand in his coat pocket with his.

"Your brother's really funny."

"I know. He could do stand-up comedy."

"I wouldn't expect that, coming from what I know of your childhood."

"He has a sense of humor *because* of our childhood. It was his coping mechanism. In the darkest times, he was always looking for a way to laugh."

For several minutes we were both silent, listening to the whispering breeze and the break of the surf.

"Was it hard for you when he got married?" I asked.

"No. I was glad for him. I had just come out of school, and I was trying to make it at the PR firm. I was working a lot. I was glad he had someone he loved and who loved him back."

"How did she die?"

"It was a fluke. She went in for a simple procedure on her knee. It was just an outpatient thing. That night at home she got a pulmonary embolism. She died next to him in their bed." He shook his head. "He really loved her. Even with all we went through, I think it was the worst thing to ever happen to him."

"Have *you* ever been in love before?"

"I thought I was. When I was younger, I would meet a beautiful girl and get excited and think, this is the one. The thing is, I didn't know what love was, or what a healthy relationship looked like, since I had never really experienced it. So the relationships never lasted.

"There was one woman I dated named Melissa. Everyone called her Missy. She was a goodhearted person, much better than I deserved. I was madly in love with her, at least I thought I was, but still I kept breaking her heart. Then, one day, I let her down one too many times. I remember looking into her eyes and seeing the pain I'd caused her. I felt shameful.

She asked, 'Lee, do you love me?' I said, 'You know I do.' She said, 'No, I don't.' Then she asked the hard question. 'Do you know what love is?' I said, 'Everyone knows what love is. You know it when you feel it.' She said, 'No. Love isn't something you feel. It's something you're willing to give. I hope you understand that someday.' Then she said goodbye.

"I didn't realize how much she meant to me until she left. I was heartbroken for a long time, because I knew that I had lost something very special. I finally just gave up. I felt like I was competing in a game where I didn't know the rules.

"That was a few years before my first book. Then, at one of my early book signings, an elderly couple came in. The man looked like he was healthy, but she was in a wheelchair, paralyzed from the neck down. He told me that she had been paralyzed in a skiing accident almost twenty years earlier. He said she liked my books and wanted to meet me. They were celebrating her birthday by coming to my book signing. Then they were going to go home and read together.

She looked at him with incredible admiration. People come to book signings excited to meet the author, the star, but he was clearly her star.

"When I opened the book, he had already signed it, *To Patricia. In all the ways.*"

"I asked him what that meant. He said, 'Mr. Harper, I thought I loved her forty years ago. But it took me forty years to learn all the ways I could show her.'"

"That's really sweet," I said.

He nodded. "That's when it occurred to me that he was happy, not because of what she could do for him, but because of what he could do for her. It was a huge epiphany for me. How many ways can you love someone? I remember thinking, these people have it right. That's what I want.

"From then on, I wanted to be that man. I wanted to learn to love like that. I wanted to learn to love someone in all the ways."

We stopped walking and he looked at me. His eyes showed his sincerity. "You asked me why I never got married. It's because up to that point, I dated people I didn't want to be married to. I was dating people just like me."

"And me?"

"When I first met you, there was something about you that reminded me of Missy. You look alike. But when I saw your *so it goes* tattoo, I couldn't believe it. I wondered if it was fate."

"Why?"

"Missy and I had this inside joke. When something bad would happen, she would look at me and say in this cute, low voice, 'So it goes.' It was like, yeah, bad things happen but it's okay. We'll be okay.

"You had that same look in your eyes when you told me about the men who hurt you. Men like me. I thought, maybe there could be a second chance to do it right. To love right. Maybe I could love someone in all the ways."

We were quiet again. Then I said, "You're doing a very good job."

"Thank you."

We started walking again. I leaned into him, and he put his arm around me as we walked back toward the house. I wanted to *be* loved like this for the rest of my life. I wanted to love like this for the rest of my life. I wanted to love in all the ways.

CHAPTER

TWENTY-SIX

And just like that, I'm homeless.

Beth Stilton's Diary

More books are sold on Black Friday than any other day of the year, which was why Lee was up before I was and back at work. He started at five in the morning doing phone-in interviews on radio stations around the US. He had his first break after noon.

I made him lunch from Thanksgiving leftovers—a turkey and cranberry sandwich on a cold dinner roll, sweet potatoes and stuffing, with a piece of pumpkin pie.

"They've got me scheduled so tight," he said. "I had to go to the bathroom at nine thirty and couldn't go until ten fifteen. I think they forget I'm human."

"You're not. You're superhuman. You're J. D. Harper."

"My bladder's not."

"That's why you've got all these bathrooms."

After lunch we went to his room and took a nap together. When I woke, he was watching me.

"How long have you been awake?" I asked.

"A little while. You still haven't told me what you want for Christmas."

"You already got me something. Remember? Tiffany?"

"That was just warming up for the season."

"Tiffany isn't warming up, it's the finish line. It's a mile past the finish line. I don't need anything. Except you."

"Now I want to buy you even more."

"Okay, you really want to give me something?"

"Yes."

"Do I have a limit?"

"Sky's the limit."

"You're going to regret this."

"Try me."

"I want a story. A short story."

"I'll dedicate a whole book to you. Then the whole world will know what you mean to me."

"I don't want it to be for the world. I want a story just for me. I know that's asking a lot, but it doesn't have to be long. It can be a couple pages, like O. Henry."

He thought for a moment, then said, "Okay. I'll write you a story."

"Now tell me what you want," I said.

"I have everything I need."

"That's not an acceptable answer." Just then my phone rang. I looked down at it. It was my friend Frankie.

"Hi, Frankie. Happy holidays."

"Not so happy," Frankie said, her voice practically dripping with misery.

"What's wrong?"

"Just be glad you didn't come for Thanksgiving. Arlo decided to deep-fry a turkey for Thanksgiving, and he caught the house on fire. The kitchen and dining room are no more."

"Was anyone hurt?"

"Not yet, but I still might kill Arlo. We're staying at a hotel right now."

"I'm so sorry. What can I do to help?"

"Unfortunately, more than you'll want to. Our builder came by this morning. He says it's going to take about six months to make the house livable. So we need to move back into the little house."

"You want me to move out?"

Lee looked at me with a concerned expression.

"It's just for six months. Then you can come back."

I breathed out heavily. "When do you need me out?"

"Ideally next Friday."

"A week from today?"

"Yeah. I'm sorry. But this whole thing is a mess. You know, Arlo's stuff isn't moving, and we're not charging you enough rent to pay for another place to live."

"I understand. You might as well save the money you're wasting on a hotel and move in right now. You probably need new furniture anyway. When I get back into town, I'll get my things out."

"Thank you. I'm really sorry to do this to you."

"I'm sorrier for what you're going through. I'll talk to you later." I hung up my phone. I looked at Lee. "I'm homeless."

"You're being evicted?"

"Frankie and Arlo need to move back in for six months. She gave me a week to move out."

His brow fell. "A week? They can't just evict you like that."

"They're not evicting me, they just asked me to let them have their home back for a while. She's been good to me. We used to split the rent, but when she moved out and I wanted the whole house, she didn't increase my rent at all. I owe her." I raked my hand back through my hair. "What a nightmare."

"Why do they need to move back?"

"Her husband decided to deep-fry a turkey for Thanksgiving."

"Bad idea."

"Very. He caught their house on fire. Now they need someplace to live while their home is repaired. They say I can move back in when the work is done." I groaned. "How am I going to find an apartment in less than a week?"

"You work from home, don't you?"

"Mostly. I have to go into the office once a month, but that's nothing."

"Then why don't you stay here?"

"In this house?"

"Why not? It's practically empty. You've got your own office, an indoor swimming pool, a house cleaner. You can drive the Mustang. You'll save all that rent money. What could possibly be wrong with that?"

"You're talking about moving in together?"

"No, it's not like that. It's not permanent, and I'm gone most of the time. And when I'm not on the road, I'll want to be with you anyway."

"What will Marc think?"

"He'll be fine. More than fine. He'll be glad for the company."

"Are you sure?"

"It's the perfect solution."

"Thank you so much. I'll have to get my things from home."

"What do you need?"

I thought about it. "Not much, really. I guess I don't need my furniture. Really just the rest of my winter clothes."

"I'll send a truck to get what you need here, the rest you can move into a storage shed. What do you think?"

"I think you're too generous." I grinned. "What if *People* magazine finds out you have a kept woman?"

He likewise grinned. "If there's one thing we know in Boston, it's that scandal sells books."

CHAPTER

TWENTY-SEVEN

I find nothing good in goodbyes. Romanticized as it is, my heart still hurts.

Beth Stilton's Diary

On Saturday, Lee had an evening book signing in Boston at the Brattle Theatre for the Harvard Bookstore—an independent bookstore with an impressive history of attracting well-known and often controversial authors, including John Updike, Salman Rushdie, Al Gore, and Stephen King.

With holiday traffic, the drive took us more than two hours, so we were rushed to pre-sign the books that were sold with the tickets. Carlie was there to meet us at the door. I hadn't seen her since dinner at Keens in New York, and she seemed uncomfortable. Maybe I was imagining it, but it seemed like she carried an air of defeat. At least that's how it felt.

Carlie and I flapped the books for Lee as he quickly signed them, and they were reboxed for distribution by the bookstore staff.

The format of the event was an onstage discussion with an interviewer, Dr. Barry James, a Harvard literature professor who was fixated on discussing the impact of the over-commercialization of literature and what he called the "Oprah effect" on the reading public.

I sat alone, secluded in the wings of the stage, hidden from the audience, but with a direct eyeline with Lee. During the presentation he kept looking at me and winking.

The crowd loved him, and the discussion concluded with a lengthy standing ovation. It all felt a little surreal. After spending so much intimate time alone with him I had allowed myself to conveniently forget that he was still a public figure—someone I had to share with the rest of the world.

After the event, Lee, Carlie, and I had dinner at Legal Seafood in Boston, then Lee and I drove back to the Cape. We had taken his Mercedes sedan, which dampened the noise of the road. We didn't talk much on the way. I don't know what he was thinking, but I had a lot on my mind. Finally, Lee said, "You're quiet tonight."

"Sorry. I'm just thinking about you leaving tomorrow. I hate it."

"It's going to be hard leaving you."

"I wish I were going with you."

"If it wasn't such a hard stretch, I'd bring you. What did you think of the event?"

"Everyone loved you. As usual. It was good to see Carlie."

He glanced over. "Was it?"

"Not really."

He grinned. "She seemed a little subdued."

"She was acting like a whipped puppy."

He laughed. "Yeah. She was."

More silence.

"Are you going to be okay cleaning out your rental by yourself?"

"I'm not by myself," I said. "You hired people. And Frankie's coming over to help."

"You're driving your car back?"

"It will be cheaper than storing it. And we won't need a moving truck. I don't really have that much to bring back. Besides that, I get nervous driving your Mustang. I feel like I'm driving a museum piece."

"It's not that expensive."

"It's not just a collector's car, it was your father's."

"True. A father I never knew." He glanced over his shoulder, then changed lanes. "What are you going to do while I'm gone?"

"Miss you."

He smiled. "It's a nice kind of pain."

I reclined the seat and closed my eyes. "What's so nice about it?"

"Parting is such sweet sorrow."

"Sounds like something a writer would say."

CHAPTER

TWENTY – EIGHT

Marc is as complex as a Rubik's cube. I was never good with Rubik's cubes.

Beth Stilton's Diary

Lee left Sunday morning. I had taken over the cooking, and I made us waffles with strawberries for breakfast. Marc came down and joined us before I drove Lee to the airport and saw him off. My heart ached. He would be gone for sixteen days. It seemed like an eternity.

Three hours later, I went back to the airport for my own flight home. Marc had told Lee that he would get me to the airport, "get" being the operative word. He booked an Uber. I didn't take it personally. He was a recluse.

Frankie picked me up in Lancaster and took me to the house. It was strange seeing their things in there with mine. I packed up what I planned to take back in my car, then we moved the rest to one corner of the front room. I had dinner with her and Arlo, then slept on the couch.

The next morning the movers came in a truck that was much too big for the few things I had. They transported what I had over to the storage unit Frankie had arranged for me. There wasn't much, so we were done by noon. Frankie and I got a burger, then I dropped her off at the house and went into my office. I thought they would be upset at me for all the time I'd missed, but honestly, I don't think they even noticed. I met with a few of my colleagues, then went back to the house.

Frankie was making dinner and had all sorts of questions about Lee and where I was living. I showed her pictures of the house and the view from the backyard. She just kept shaking her head and saying, "I always knew you were going places."

Tuesday morning, I said goodbye to Frankie and Arlo and drove back to the Cape. Halfway there, Lee called, and we talked for more than an hour. He had just finished a book signing at a Little Professors bookstore in Birmingham and gone back to his hotel to rest. It was lovely to hear his voice. He bemoaned the fact that so many of his favorite bookstores were gone, especially the Books-A-Million in Hoover where he'd had one of his first signings. Carlie, unfortunately, had caught Covid and flown back home to Michigan to recover. Lee's next stops were Cincinnati and Dayton.

I got back to the Cape by six. I made myself a salad, then took everything from my car into my room.

Wednesday morning, I went for a swim. Afterward, I dried off, then, still in my bathing suit, made myself some avocado toast. It was one of those days that I just didn't feel the need to get dressed. I brought my computer out to the main room and signed back in to work. The house felt so empty without Lee around.

After work I went through the house library looking for something to read. Lee had an eclectic collection, from century-old classics to advanced readers copies that hadn't been released to the public yet. There were two entire rows of his books, some in languages I didn't recognize. I picked up one of them to see if I could figure out where it was from.

"That one's in Farsi," Marc said, startling me. "That's Iran."

"How are you?" I asked. "I haven't seen you for a while."

"It's how I roll," he said. "Now you see me, now you don't." He looked me over. "Are you going swimming?"

"No. I went this morning. I just never bothered to get dressed."

"Oh," he said. I couldn't tell what he thought of that. "Have you talked to Al today?"

"Not today. We talked yesterday for an hour."

"You talked a whole hour? About what?"

"Life on the road and things . . ."

"Things," he said.

"So, Lee's books are in Iran?"

"Not legally. The US doesn't have copyright agreements with Iran, so they just take them. We don't get royalties."

"That's not good."

"It's no big deal. We're doing okay."

"How many countries are Lee's books in?"

"Laurie would know that. We count languages instead of countries. Last count, we were translated into forty-three different languages. Have you read them all?"

"All the languages?"

"No. All his books. In English."

"Yes. More than once."

"And?"

"I love them. That's why I'm here."

"You're here because he loves you."

I smiled at the thought. "You're right."

"Do you have a favorite of the books?"

"I loved them all. I think *Jacob's Ladder* was his best critical work, but if I had to choose just one, I'd say *Bethel*. That's the book that saved my life."

"You mean figuratively, of course."

"No, literally. It was a really hard time in my life. That book spoke to me. It gave me hope."

He nodded. "Do you remember what part?"

"It was when he got to the city line and looked back and realized that nothing was really holding him to his past. There was a line about the shackles we wear."

"'The greatest shackles we wear are those forged by our own fears.'"

"That's it," I said. "It gave me hope."

"You like to read."

"I always have."

"Have you read Steinbeck?"

"I read *The Grapes of Wrath*."

"*Grapes of Wrath, Cannery Row, Of Mice and Men, East of Eden, The Winter of our Discontent*. He wrote some remarkable books."

"I'll have to look into them."

"Just a minute," Marc said. He ran up the stairs, returning a moment later with two books. They had leather covers, and the titles were imprinted in gold. "*Of Mice and Men* helped inspire *Bethel*." He handed me one of the books. "You can read it."

I took the book from him. "These are nice. They're leather."

"They're just slipcases to protect them."

"This book inspired *Bethel*?"

"*Helped*," Marc said.

I opened the cover. On the title page was a signature.

"That's not really John Steinbeck's signature, is it?"

"Yes, it's a signed first edition."

I tried to give it back to him, but he just put his hands in his pockets.

"I'm not going to read this copy. I shouldn't even be touching it."

"What good is a book if you don't read it? It's a short read. You'll notice the impact this little book had on popular culture. Steinbeck was a very powerful writer."

"I'll be careful with it."

"This one is my favorite of Steinbeck's works, *East of Eden*. Steinbeck considered it his magnum opus. He said everything he'd written up to that point was practice. He didn't win any major awards for it, but he should have."

"Is it autographed too?"

"No. I still haven't found one of those." He handed me the book. "But it's also a first edition. I think you'll enjoy it."

"Thank you. I'll have lots of time to read now that Lee's gone." I looked at him more closely. "What do you do when he's gone?"

He didn't answer me for a moment, then he said, "Same thing I do when he's here."

"And what is that?"

"A lot of reading."

"Maybe someday you'll write a book too."

"Maybe," he said. He looked me over again, then said, "You should probably wear clothes."

"Sorry. I'll do that."

He walked back up the stairs. I wondered when I would see him again.

CHAPTER

TWENTY-NINE

The first book Marc gave me was Steinbeck's Of Mice and Men—*the story of two men who care for each other. The second was Steinbeck's* East of Eden—*about the conflict between two brothers. If he's trying to tell me something, I have no idea what it is.*

Beth Stilton's Diary

The strangest thing about living in the house without Lee in it was that I was both always alone and never alone, if you know what I mean. Marc was like a phantom, and I never knew when he would appear. I think he had said the thing about being dressed in case I got lax and started walking through the house in my underwear. Or less.

It was several days after he gave me the books before he showed up again. I was in the kitchen making lunch when he walked up to me.

"Have you seen my mood ring?"

"Your mood ring? No."

"I lost my mood ring. I don't know how I feel about that."

I shook my head. "I don't know when you're being serious or not."

"Usually not," he said. "I told my wife that she drew her eyebrows too high. She looked surprised."

"That was funny."

"Thank you. Have you read the books I gave you?"

"I read *Of Mice and Men*."

"Did you like it?"

"Very much. I'm curious about how it inspired Lee to write *Bethel*."

"Two men, one sharing his dream of a better world."

"I see that. Hope."

He nodded. "Let me know when you finish the other."

"*East of Eden* is considerably longer. That will take a while."

"I won't be timing you."

"Thank you. And I had a question. Do you decorate for Christmas?"

"We usually have some bearded guys come and put up the outside lights. I don't know if Lee remembered to hire them this year. You should ask him."

"How about inside the house? Do you have any decorations?"

"In the garage, there are two tubs. They're on the red shelves on the north end. They're black with yellow tops. They're marked *XMAS*."

"I think I can find those. Would you like to decorate with me?"

"Not really. But you can on this floor."

"Just down here," I said. "Thank you."

"You'll need help getting the bins down. They're heavy. I'll help you with that."

We walked across the yard to the garage. I had never been inside, since Lee always parked his cars out front or, at least, picked me up there.

"The code is 4455," Marc said as he punched it in on the keypad next to the first bay. The door opened, exposing a beautiful cherry-red car with a chrome grille, four chrome headlamps, and tall, spoked tires.

"That may be the most beautiful car I've ever seen."

"It's a 1935 Duesenberg SSJ. It's worth about three million

dollars." He looked at me. "It's part of Lee's collection. I collect pewter soldier figurines and books. He collects cars."

We walked into the garage. Marc was right, I wouldn't have been able to get the bins down. As he pulled one from the shelf I noticed a long burn mark on his arm, similar to the ones I'd seen on Lee's back. There were at least a dozen smaller round marks as well. He noticed me looking and held my gaze until I looked away.

He got the other bin down, then retrieved a hand truck, stacked the bins on top of each other, and pushed them over to the house.

"Will you shut the garage?" he said to me. "Just push the enter button."

"Sure."

Before shutting the door, I took one last glance at the beautiful car. I wanted Lee to take me for a ride in it.

"Clive Cussler collected Duesenbergs," Marc said. "He had more than a hundred and eighty cars when he died. So one isn't that many." He pushed the bins inside to the kitchen, where he took them off the cart. "There you go."

"Thank you."

"No worries." He started for the stairs, then stopped. "The scars you saw on my arm are from my mother. She liked to put her cigarettes out on me." Before I could say anything, he was gone.

CHAPTER

THIRTY

In times like these, the height of our previous joy is revealed by the sudden depth of our misery.

Beth Stilton's Diary

The next days passed quickly. I followed Lee online through Montgomery, Birmingham, Cincinnati, Dayton, Indianapolis, Denver, Salt Lake City, Phoenix, then ending in Dallas–Fort Worth and Houston. Texas. I called Pauline to let her know that I'd be missing book club on the eighth. She was excited to hear where I was.

"So you're shacking up with him now?"

"I'm just watching the house while he's gone on book tour."

"Sure you are, you little coquette," she said. "I'll let the Babes know. And darling, you've got this." I loved the woman.

The morning of the fourteenth, I woke as giddy as a child on Christmas morning. Lee called me around eight.

"I'm coming home."

"I'm counting the seconds. What time?"

"I land at five seventeen at Gateway."

"I'll be there."

"I've got to run. I'll see you soon."

My heart was doing the monkey dance. (Whatever that is.) My author was finally coming home. Despite his multitude of eccentricities, I had, for the most part, enjoyed the time I had with Marc. I couldn't help but wonder where he would be without Lee, but I also saw him as his staunchest defender and most loyal ally.

As it was our last day alone, I wanted to talk to him about the book he had loaned me, *East of Eden*. I had finished it just a few days earlier. Like the first book, it was a story of two men, but in this case they were two brothers, an allegory of Cain and Abel. There was serious tension between the two. I wondered what part of that story he connected with.

I wanted to return it, because I was nervous holding his first edition. Out of curiosity I had looked up its value and priced it at more than six thousand dollars.

I got the book from my room to return to him, then walked to the foot of the stairs and called him. "Marc."

Nothing. I never knew if he was home. I called for him again but still no reply. I decided just to leave the book at the top of the stairway, but then leaving the valuable book on the ground didn't feel right. What if he stepped on it?

I admit now that curiosity played a part. I wondered what the inner sanctum looked like. I had seen him come from the door at the top of the stairway carrying papers, so I assumed it was his office. I looked both ways, then opened the door. I couldn't believe what was inside.

The room was as out of place in the home's motif as a doughnut stand at a WeightWatchers conference. Where the rest of the home was uniformly traditional Cape Cod design, this room looked like it had been plucked from a Victorian mansion. The room was dark, and its only ambient light came from a ceiling-mounted stained-glass window.

To my left was a Victorian-style mahogany parlor settee with tufted red wine velvet, and to my right was a small table with a display case of pewter Civil War figurines.

The ceiling was the same dark wood as the walls and was elegantly coffered, rendering the room contrary to the rest of the house: dark, enclosed, and cozy. Two brass-and-alabaster light fixtures hung from the ceiling, giving the room its primary light.

The wall opposite the entrance had a marble-fronted fireplace with a dark rosewood mantel and tile hearth, with large brass andirons. A flickering fire was burning in the box.

Above the mantel were two, dim electric sconces that flanked a large, gilded-frame oil painting of a woman's portrait, which, from her contemporary dress, I guessed to be Marc's wife.

The side walls were floor-to-ceiling bookshelves with brass rails and rolling ladders on each side. In the center of the room was a kidney-shaped wooden writing desk with an inlaid gilded-leather writing pad and ball-and-claw feet. There was a laptop computer on the desk surrounded by papers.

Most peculiar were the hoarder-like stacks of paper around the room that climbed upward from the floor like parchment stalagmites. One stack rose more than four feet.

I walked closer to examine one of the paper columns. The stacks were composed of handwritten book manuscripts neatly, if precariously, stacked on top of each other. The writing was beautiful calligraphy. I knew it wasn't Lee's scrawl. I lifted the top sheet of the nearest column. In beautiful lettering were the words

Jacob's Ladder
A Novel

There were myriad marks and scratches on the manuscripts, entire sections written in the elegant calligraphy. My heart began to beat faster. I went to another one of the stacks and lifted the top page.

My Brother's Keeper
A Novel

"No," I said to myself. I didn't believe what I was seeing. These were handwritten manuscripts, nine stacks in all. I set the book I'd brought on the desk, then examined the stack closest to it. There, on top of the pile, were the words I feared most to see. It was what I didn't want to see.

Bethel

Erased, but still etched in the paper, were the words:

Marcus Lee Heller

A sickness rose in my gut as tears welled up in my eyes. "It can't be." Just then Marc walked into the room, holding a mug of beer, completely oblivious to my presence. He froze when he saw me, his face looking as shaken as if he'd walked in on a crime in progress.

"What are you doing in here?"

My heart stopped. "I was bringing your book back. I wanted to talk to you about it."

His eyes revealed his panic. "You can't be in here."

"I called for you. I was . . ." I held a page in my trembling hand. "What are these?"

"You need to leave."

"Did you write these books?" Tears began to fall down my cheeks. "Tell me you didn't write these books."

He just looked back at me.

I stepped toward him. "You wrote all of these books, didn't you?"

His eyes revealed what I didn't want to believe.

"You need to leave now," he said. "You need to go home."

"Not until I see him. I need to hear it from his own mouth."

"You need to hear what?" he asked, his voice hardening.

"That he lied to me."

"Is that going to make you feel better?"

"No," I said softly. "Nothing will do that."

CHAPTER

THIRTY-ONE

It is time for me to leave. I should have waited to unpack my emotional suitcase.

Beth Stilton's Diary

My feelings had done a complete flip-flop since the morning, and my unbridled excitement to see Lee had turned to crushing dread. Lee's words to me, "You can trust me," echoed in a mocking refrain. I'd been living a fiction. The man I loved was a fiction too. The worst part was, I didn't know who I had fallen in love with. I'd loved the words, but they were Marc's. And I wasn't in love with Marc.

I packed my car, then waited in my room for Lee's return. Marc picked him up from the airport. I assumed that Marc would tell him what happened, but in his typical, enigmatic form, he hadn't said anything other than I didn't want to pick him up.

I heard the door open and Lee's footsteps in the hall as he walked directly to my room. He knocked once on my door, then opened it. I was sitting on my bed next to my suitcase. His face was tight with distress as he looked back and forth from the suitcase to me.

"What are you doing?"

"I'm going home."

"You don't have a home.'"

"Then I'm just leaving."

His expression grew even more perplexed. "This morning you were practically giddy that I was coming home. What's going on?"

"I found out the truth. You didn't write those books."

He gazed at me as the reality sunk in, then he lightly groaned. "That."

"Yes, *that*."

"Marc told you?"

"I discovered it on my own."

He exhaled loudly. "I need to explain."

"What's there to explain? You stole your brother's books. You stole his words."

"It's not that simple."

"No, it is. You said I could trust you."

"You still can. Just let me explain."

I crossed my arms across my chest. "Okay. Explain why you lied to me."

"After Marc's wife died, he broke down. After all we had been through growing up, he had miraculously found his match, and they started to build a life with a hope of happiness. Then he lost the only woman he had ever loved.

"He just gave up. He stopped going to work, he stopped paying his bills. It was as if he had stopped living as well. He was deep in debt, and now he had his wife's college debt and massive medical bills. His creditors took everything.

"At the time, I was barely making it myself, living in a basement apartment in West End, when Marc called me from a pay phone and said he was homeless. I brought him home. On top of everything else, I was now paying for him too. He still wouldn't work. He started drinking and stopped leaving the house, except to buy booze.

"The bills were piling up and my payments were getting

later and later. One day, out of frustration, I asked him what he did all day. He went his room and brought out a stack of papers and dropped it on the table. He said, 'I wrote a book.' Then he went back into his room.

"His manuscript was completely handwritten. As I went through it I noticed tearstains on some of the pages. That's how he was trying to deal with his grief. He was writing it out.

"The book he wrote was called *Bethel*. I started reading it and couldn't believe what he'd written. I was a literature major. I knew good writing. And this was nothing short of genius. I stayed up all night and read it.

"The next morning, I told him that he needed to publish it. He flatly refused. He didn't want anyone to read it.

"But we were desperate. It was just a matter of time before the world I was propping up was going to fall in on us. So, without him knowing, I got one of our interns at work to type up the manuscript, then I started calling agents. Of course, no one would talk to me.

"Then, call it fate, but on one of the last phone numbers I had, I got a hit. A junior agent working late answered the phone. It was Laurie. She asked me to email her the book, and she called the next day. The first words out of her mouth were, 'This may be the most brilliant work to ever come across my desk.'"

"Does Laurie know you didn't write the book?" I asked.

"Of course."

"Then she's part of it."

"What's '*it*'?"

"The charade."

He ignored my dig. "Laurie sent me a representation contract from her agency. I was excited. I thought Marc would be excited. I took the contract to him to sign. I wasn't trying to take his book or his money, I was trying to help him get back on his feet. But he didn't see it that way. He was angry that I had shared his story. He tore up the contract and walked out of the house.

"The next day he came back and apologized. He'd written a letter gifting me all the rights to the book. But on one condition. That he was never, in any way, to be attached to it. That was the deal. I would have to claim it as my own. It was his idea. Not mine.

"Laurie sent out the book. There was a lot of buzz. Seven publishers wanted it. It ended up going into an auction. The high bid was two million dollars for a two-book deal. It saved us. It saved my brother. Everything just snowballed from there."

"You said it was your book."

"It is my book. He gave it to me."

"I don't care whose book it is legally. I care that you lied to me."

"I never lied to you."

"You lied to me in the worst way possible. I told you that I fell in love with your words. But they weren't yours. You knew they weren't yours. And you never told me."

"I never said they were my words."

"You never said they weren't."

He breathed out slowly. "No, I didn't."

The room fell into silence. For what seemed an eternity we just sat there. Then I noticed the tears in his eyes.

"Don't worry. I won't tell anyone your secret."

"That's not what I'm worried about," he said. "Please, don't leave. I love you."

Even though my heart was breaking, I turned the pain into anger. I said, "I thought I was in love with you. But I guess I was in love with someone else the whole time."

I took my suitcase and walked out of the house.

Lee didn't follow me. As I got to my car I looked up and saw Marc looking out at me from his second-story window. His face was emotionless. I got into my car and drove off. I started crying again as soon as I left the property.

CHAPTER

THIRTY - TWO

I can't get him out of my mind. Or is it my heart that he refuses to leave?

Beth Stilton's Diary

I was too tired and emotional to make the drive home, so I spent the night in Worcester at a Holiday Inn Express. Not exactly the Mark. As I lay in bed, I realized that I was living my childhood again—alone, afraid, and homeless. My night terrors returned.

The next day I drove all the way home to Lancaster, except I didn't have a home there anymore, so I drove to the house to see my only friend. Frankie was surprised to see me.

"You're back? Why are you back?"

"I left Lee."

She tried to look sympathetic, but I'm sure she thought I was an imbecile. "Why?"

"He lied to me."

"Was it another woman?"

"No."

"Well, whatever it was, I'm sure you know what you're doing. I'm here for you. Do you need a place to stay?"

"Just for tonight, if I can."

"Of course you can. You can sleep with me. Arlo can sleep on the couch."

"You're still mad at him?"

"It's going to take a while."

The next day I went out apartment hunting. There wasn't

much in my price range, but I found a dingy little studio apartment with a month-to-month lease.

The next few weeks I immersed myself in work, grabbing as much overtime as I could, which was always easy to get during the holidays. The season moved around me like a parade, and I was the person on the sidewalk watching it go by.

All the while I was trying to get Lee out of my mind. When he had come for me after I left him in New York, he said that my face was graffitied on his mind. Now it was my turn. It didn't help that his book was still the number one book in America. I couldn't go into any bookstore or grocery store and not see him. I turned on the television once and saw him being interviewed.

Worst of all, the further I got from it all, the harder it was for me to defend my actions. I had acted rashly from fear. The reality was that everything Lee said had made sense. Under the circumstances any reasonable person would have done the same. He was trying to help his brother pull his life together. He wasn't trying to deceive anyone. He wasn't trying to hurt anyone.

But I had. I had hurt the only man I'd ever known who had shown me real love. It was painful to accept my culpability. And I had already gotten a second chance. I knew there was no way back.

CHAPTER

THIRTY-THREE

It is never pleasant to look through the glass of offense and find yourself looking back.

Beth Stilton's Diary

I t was three days before Christmas. I was in bed with a cold when the doorbell rang. I ignored it and it rang again. Then again. Then again. Finally, I got up angry, put on my robe, and walked to the front. I yanked open the door ready to rail on whoever was there.

Incredibly, Marc was standing at my door.

"Hi," he said calmly. He looked out of place. It was hard to picture him away from the property, let alone Massachusetts.

"How did you find me?"

"I went to your old place." He held up a necklace. "I bought some sea glass from a hippie-looking guy, and a fish sculpture made of driftwood. I don't think he sells many of them. But it's a fish. It might look good at the house. If not, we'll make a fire in the pit with it."

"Arlo told you where I was," I said.

"That's his name. Like the folk singer. May I come in?"

I sighed. "Why not?"

He brushed the snow off his shoulders, then stepped inside, shutting the door behind him.

"May I take your coat?"

"No." He shrugged it off, folded it in half over his arm, and just held it. He looked around my pathetic ugly apartment. "Nice place."

"No, it's not. Do you want something to drink? Something hot?"

"Do you have mulled wine?"

"No."

"What about a hot buttered rum with one of those little cinnamon sticks?"

"I'm sorry. I don't have anything like that. I have powdered hot chocolate I can put in the microwave."

"I don't want that."

"Whatever, have a seat."

Marc looked around at his seating options, then perched reluctantly on my couch.

"You don't like to wear clothes, do you."

"I'm sick. You got me out of bed."

"Oh. I'm sorry. You got me out of Massachusetts."

"You should have told me you were coming," I said. "I could have made dinner for you."

"I didn't come to eat. I would have gone someplace nice."

"Your brother sent you?"

He kept looking around my place, like he was trying to find a way out. He turned back to me. "No, he doesn't know I'm here. He's back out on the road."

"I thought he was done with his tour."

"He was." Characteristically, without warning he launched into the conversation. "You're not right."

"What?"

"You're not right. Leaving Al wasn't right. You're not being fair."

"*I'm* not being fair? At least I'm not a liar."

"Yes, you are. You're one of the biggest liars I know."

"How dare you?"

"That wasn't really daring, I was just telling the truth. Isn't that why Al came and got you the first time, because you were lying to yourself that you weren't worthy of him? Everyone lies. Some lie to protect themselves; some lie to hurt themselves. No difference."

"I don't care why he lied."

He looked perplexed. "Why?"

I didn't know how to answer that. "I told Lee that I loved him because of what he wrote in *Bethel*. It was you who wrote the words that reached me. Not him."

"Then if you're honest, you should be in love with me."

He had a point.

"Do you know where Bethel is?" He asked it like he had forgotten our conversation and was now looking for directions.

"It's thirty miles north of here."

"Not the one in Pennsylvania. The one in the book."

"No. You're vague about it. It could be anywhere."

"That's because it doesn't exist. Not on any map. It only exists in Al."

"What do you mean?"

"As children, there were times our mother would beat us so severely that it would be hours before we even dared move. During those times, Al would rub my back, then tell me a story about a place called Bethel. It was a place where people were kind, and mothers and fathers were good to their children. There would always be enough to eat because ice cream bars grew on trees. And children forgot how to cry because there was no reason to.

"I asked him where Bethel was. He said it was close. Very close. And one day, he would take me there." He looked me in the eyes. "Do you even know what the word *Bethel* means?"

I shook my head. "No."

"It means 'the House of God.' That's what Al created for me, for my mind. He gave me my own religion. He gave me a place I could have hope." Marc was quiet for a moment, then he said, "I know you've seen the burns on his back. Do you know where they came from?"

"They came from your mother."

"Do you know why?"

I shook my head. "No."

"It was my fault. When I was seven, I found my mother's cigarettes. I wanted to be big like her. So I tried to smoke them. But each time I'd choke on it then spit it out of my mouth. Then I'd light another one.

"I caught the carpet on fire. It could have been a big fire, but Al came in. He stomped on the fire, then covered it with a blanket and put it out. But there was already a big hole in the carpet and the room was filled with smoke. The smell was like burnt rubber. It filled the room.

"That's when my mother walked in. She was going out that night, so she was dressed in her skanky dress and her hair was done up. As usual, she had been drinking. She had that look of hell in her eyes, that crazy, mad look that turned our blood cold.

"She shouted at us, 'What did you do?'

"I had never been so afraid in my life. I thought, this time she'll kill me. I knew she would.

"But before I could say anything, Al turned to my mother and said, 'I'm sorry, Mommy. I didn't mean to start the fire. I won't ever smoke your cigarettes again. I promise.'

"She glanced at me, then she went after him with a rage I'd never seen before. She beat him with her fists until he was bloody.

"Then she got this sadistic, gleeful look in her eyes and said, 'You like to burn things?' She went out of the room, then came back with her curling iron. She lifted his shirt, then pressed her knee into the small of his back so he couldn't move.

"Then she pressed the iron against him. It sizzled against his skin. I could smell his flesh burn. He screamed in pain. I shouted at her to stop. I even ran at her, but she pushed me away with the iron. That's when I got that big scar on my arm you saw. But she wouldn't stop. She was hell-bent on making him pay. I wanted to tell her it was my fault, but I was a coward.

"But Al never told on me. She just kept pressing the iron against him over and over until it wasn't hot enough to burn anymore. Then she threw it against the wall, pointed at me, and said, 'If you ever light a match in my house, you'll get the same.' Then she got up and left.

"I just looked at my brother. His eyes were glazed, and I couldn't tell if he was alive or dead. He was in shock. His back was one massive blister.

"He didn't move all that night. He would groan lightly, then he would suddenly be silent. Several times I was sure he had died. My mother had come home in the middle of the night drunk and fallen asleep on the couch. I wanted to kill her. I was only seven years old, and I felt that much hate. But I hated myself even more than I hated her. Because it was my fault.

"The next morning, she got up, hungover. She must have remembered what she had done, because she came into the room mumbling, holding a beer can against her head and a brown bottle of something, probably hydrogen peroxide, that she poured on his back. It just foamed up. He groaned but didn't move or speak. A couple hours later she came back in and put a big piece of gauze over his back and said, 'If anyone asks what happened, tell them you fell asleep against the radiator.'

"The next night I asked him to tell me stories about Bethel, but he wouldn't. He never spoke of Bethel again. That's why I wrote the book. I wanted to believe again. I wanted him to believe again."

To my surprise, Marc's eyes suddenly filled with tears. "The only reason I could write about Bethel was because Al lived it. He taught me what it meant to love. You keep saying that you fell in love with my words—like they *magically* saved your life. What are words? They're cheap. Anyone can give words. Lies are words. Insults are words. Al showed me what love really was. He lived Bethel. He was Bethel.

"You decide, do you want words, or do you want the real thing? Because that's what this is about. That's all this is about.

"He covered for me when I burned the carpet, he covered for me when I wrote a book. It's no different. You think you're better than him? Yeah, right. His whole life he's been hurt by the people he loves. People like you and me. Welcome to the club, baby." He stood and walked to the door. "That's all I have to say. Merry Christmas." He put on his jacket, then opened the door.

"Marc."

He turned back. "What?"

"Where is he?"

"He's out doing what I didn't have the courage to do."

"Where?"

"No idea. Look it up," he said, walking out my door.

CHAPTER

THIRTY – FOUR

Such grace is undeserved. But then, grace deserved, is no longer grace.

Beth Stilton's Diary

DECEMBER 22

It wasn't hard to find him. His publisher's publicity team made sure of that. He was at a bookstore in Indianapolis, then would move on to Fort Wayne, Indiana, before ending his tour. It was just three days before Christmas, and the flights were slammed. To make things worse, there was a storm in Minneapolis that shut down flights across the US, leaving thousands stranded.

I got bumped off my flight to Indianapolis, then, after waiting in the airport for six hours, my replacement flight to Fort Wayne was cancelled.

An exhausted but sympathetic airline employee suggested that I take the last seat on a flight to Dayton, Ohio, and figure out how to get to Fort Wayne from there.

It was going to be close. I had trouble finding an Uber who would drive that far, and by the time I found someone, I was afraid I was going to miss the signing. But I had to try.

It was a quarter to nine when I arrived at the bookstore in Fort Wayne. To my relief, there was still a line of maybe fifty people. I grabbed a book and walked to the back of the line. A bookstore woman intercepted me.

"I'm sorry, ma'am, we cut the line off an hour ago. Mr. Harper's been signing since four."

"It's okay. He's a friend of mine."

She smiled skeptically. "I'm sorry, ma'am. The line is done."

I stood there for a moment trying to decide what to do, when I heard someone say, "It's okay, Martha. She's a friend."

I looked over. Carlie was standing on the other side of the line.

"Thank you," I said.

She managed a small smile. "Good luck."

When I got near the signing table, I could see how weary Lee was. He looked miserable. His head was down, and he was uncharacteristically focused on the books as the staff pushed the remaining books through. It was past nine and the store was closed, which was made clear when the Christmas music on the PA system abruptly stopped leaving the store in a noticeably uneasy silence.

Lee wasn't even looking up when I set my book on the table in front of him.

"Who would you like that signed . . ."

He stopped speaking when he saw me.

I was trembling. I swallowed. "I already signed it. For you."

He looked at me with sad, tired eyes. I couldn't read what he was thinking. I suddenly realized what a foolish thing I'd done in coming to him. I had treated him awfully. Twice. I didn't deserve his forgiveness. I didn't even deserve his courtesy.

"Let's see what you signed," he said, opening to the title page.

To my dearest Lee,
I don't deserve your forgiveness.
I don't deserve you.
But if you'll give me one more chance,
I'll spend the rest of my life showing you how much
I love you.
In all the ways, .
Beth

He looked at my inscription for what seemed like forever. Then he looked up, his weary eyes joining with mine.

"How would you like me to sign your book?"

I was suddenly just another fan, another reader on the other side of the table. I couldn't keep the tears from falling down my cheeks.

Everyone around us was quiet. I guessed they sensed that something unusual was happening, even if they didn't know what it was.

Lee just looked at me, waiting for my answer. Finally, I said, "I'm sorry to bother you. I'm sorry for everything. You don't need to sign it."

I reached to take back my book, but he put his hand on top of mine.

"Beth, how would you like me to sign your book?"

I took in a deep breath, then said, "Would you please sign it to Beth." I swallowed, then said, "In all the ways. And then just your signature."

He took his pen and wrote,

To my Beth.
I forgive you. I love you.
In all the ways.
Your Lee

Then he stood up and walked around the table. We kissed like no one was watching.

EPILOGUE

"Writing a book is like falling in love. You think you're pulling the strings until you discover you're really the puppet."

J. D. Harper

There is a Bible passage that reads, *He who is forgiven much, loves much.* I find great relevance in that verse. Lee has forgiven me much. Twice. The love that forgiveness fills me with is indescribable but not inexpressible. I plan to spend the rest of my life showing him just how grateful I am.

After the book signing in Fort Wayne, Lee and I flew back to the Cape to spend Christmas together. It was the first time in my life that I felt like I was home for the holiday. What Marc told me, when he revealed their family secret, has never left me. Bethel isn't a place, or even a book. It's Lee. It's always been Lee. I spent Christmas in Bethel.

I wondered how Marc would respond to my return. Of course, it was as dispassionate as if I'd just gotten back from grocery shopping. He even had a Christmas present for me — his first-edition copy of *East of Eden*. Inside he wrote a note with his usual flair.

Welcome back. Stay downstairs. Wear clothes.

Lee had a present for me as well. He wrote the story I asked him for. It's about a man who finds a bird with a broken wing and takes it home to care for it. The bird asks the man why he would choose an injured bird, when there are so many who can fly. The man tells the bird, "If it can already fly, it doesn't really need me. And in the deepest places in our hearts, we all want to be needed by someone."

After the man nursed the bird back to health, he took her to the window, held her aloft, and said, "You're free to go now. Fly away." The bird replies, "Where would I fly to, dear man?"

"Home," he says.

"Very well." The bird then alit on his shoulder. "You are my home. You are where I want to be."

It is truly our story.

We were engaged on Christmas Day. It wasn't planned or expected, but as Lee observed, the best things usually aren't. You might even say that I proposed—or at least deserve the assist.

Back in New York, when I asked Lee what he wanted for Christmas, he asked for something that money couldn't buy. After receiving his present, I told him that I had a gift for him too. I offered him me. All of me. He got a very big smile. (I think he might have been excited to unwrap his gift.)

Then he said, I suppose that means we're getting married. I said, "I might have said yes before you asked." Then I added, "It doesn't matter. I was already yours."

We were married on the Cape the following June. The media wasn't invited, but there were helicopters circling. So it goes.

Frankie was my bridesmaid. Arlo hung out by the refreshments. When he saw Marc, he said, "Hey, you're the dude who bought my Driftwood Pisces."

Marc said, "Was that the wooden fish?"

Arlo said, "Yes. Can I see where you put it?"

"We had to burn it," Marc said.

Marc, of course, was Lee's best man. He hired an armed guard to stand at the bottom of his stairs to keep anyone from wandering.

Laurie was there. "I knew this was how the story was going to end," she said.

"How is that?" I asked.

She said, "I'm an agent. It's my job to pick winners."

Carlie was there, of course. She seemed happy for us, even if she was still a little envious.

All of the Bordeaux Babes came, even Maxine, who tried to make a move on Marc. He finally said to her, "Aren't there other people here you could talk to?"

Marc did, however, introduce himself to Alice. The two of them hit it off, not that anyone observing their interactions would notice. They were as awkward as a middle school blind date. Now they talk every day. It's sweet, really. I think he gave her Arlo's sea glass bracelet. I asked him if he thought their relationship might go somewhere. He said, "You're prying."

I said, "Absolutely I am."

He said, "You mean marriage."

I said, "Yes."

He said, "January 12, 2026."

I asked him if there was any significance to that date. He said it was the fiftieth anniversary of Agatha Christie's death.

So it goes.

You're likely wondering how the writing thing is going to work out. It's like this: J. D. Harper is a brand name. Lee is going to take three years off from touring. At that time, if Marc is ready, he'll step in and take his place, ready at last to rejoin the wider world—at least behind the safety of a pen name. People already confuse the two, and in three years away, no one will notice the difference. At least physically. I can already picture Marc at a book signing. "That's too many books. You should just go away."

I told you at the beginning of my story that love should be infused with magic. Our story is magical. I am love's puppet, bound by strings of joy and love and gratitude. I can't wait to see where our story goes. Most of all, how our love grows.

In all the ways.

ACKNOWLEDGMENTS

T his book was nothing short of a miracle. Thank you to my muses who kept the story coming at all hours and assured me it was possible. 11:11

Thank you to my friend, Jaimie Aimes, who gave me the idea for this story and suffered much of what Beth has. May your dream of Operation Host reach its full potential and help myriad United States military veterans find peace and healing. Thank you for serving our country. (Go to OperationHost.org to learn more)

To Jonathan Karp. (I hope it's okay I put you in the book.)

Blessings to my publisher, The Jenz: Jen Bergstrom and Jen Long, Aimee Bell (VP, editorial director), Eliza Hanson (publishing manager), Caroline Pallotta (managing editor), Min Choi (cover art), Ali Chesnick (Abby's editorial assistant), Al Madocs (production editor), Paul O'Halloran (sub rights), Jessica Roth (publicist), and Tianna Kelly (marketing).

To my patient and wise editor, Abby Zidle, who kept the process moving through a very difficult time of my life.

To my agent, Laurie Liss, who plays herself in this book and whom this book is dedicated to.

And to my ultra patient wife, Keri, who not only cancelled our fortieth anniversary trip without complaint so I could finish this book but took good care of me while I locked myself away to finish this story. I love you in all the ways.